S F
BOOKS

Planet Scumm is a triannual short fiction anthology. Visit **planetscumm.space** for submissions.

First Printing, 2021   ISBN: 978-1-970154-08-5

© SPARK & FIZZ BOOKS
Portland | Boston | Outer Space

SPARK & FIZZ BOOKS PRESENTS

PLANET SCUMM

SUMMER 2021   "SNAKE EYES"   ISSUE NO. 11

—— A MEDUSOID TABLE OF CONTENTS ——

TRANSMISSION: SCUMM
GUEST EDITOR, HAILEY PIPER...V

AUTHOR BIOS..XI

A DEFIANCE OF VIOLINS
ANA GARDNER..1

THE HOLLOW STARS IN HEAVEN
AVERY KIT MALONE...15

HIVEMIND
LC VON HESSEN...23

THE SECRET OF THETA PI
STEPHANIE GRAY...36

THE LONG SLEEP
DIANA FENVES...45

REAL SUGAR IS HARD TO FIND
SIM KERN...61

MA DRESDEN
LAURA BARKER..76

AN EVENTUAL FEAST
LINDSAY KING-MILLER...03

EDITORIAL SPOTLIGHT...99

GUEST EDITOR-IN-CHIEF	CREATIVE DIRECTOR	GUEST EDITOR	GUEST EDITOR
HAILEY PIPER	*ALYSSA ALARCÓN SANTO*	*MAURA McGONAGLE*	*CLARE FULLER*

COVER AND SPOT ILLUSTRATIONS BY MAURA McGONAGLE | @MCMCGONAGLE | PATREON.COM/DOINGARTIGUESS

MADE WITH SUPPORT FROM THE PLANET SCUMM TEAM | *TYLER BERD, SEAN CLANCY, AND SAM RHEAUME*

GUEST EDITOR-IN-CHIEF, HAILEY PIPER

TRANSMISSION: SCUMM

So like I always say, you can't call an interplanetary flight complete without sparking an interplanetary incident. But enough about my love life, we're back!

Between paranormal paramours and swell symphonies of that sweet Earther musical instrument, the car horn, the Starship Scummy keeps on cruising the crust of this cosmic sandwich we call life. And what's a sandwich without a few ingredients? The top tales of time and space make up the bologna and cheese of life.

What's that banging sound, you ask? A desperate kind of thud, thud, thud?

That's no Martian. That's Hailey Piper floating in the airlock! Never you mind her; she isn't going anywhere. But these stories will take you places.

Chips make the world go round. Sour cream, salsa, even microchips—the tastiest kind. But in "A Defiance of Violins," Ana Gardner says them Earthers are putting chips in their skulls, getting all sorts of sensations, and not the sweet kind your buddy Scummy brings. Way too cognitive to be cool ranch.

But what was I saying about paranormal paramours and interplanetary incidents?

My love life's an uncomplicated drop in the ocean compared to the hot night life Avery Kit Malone tells us all about with *"The Hollow Stars in Heaven."*

Speaking of oceans, how about that Big Apple dipping into the Atlantic? Am I pronouncing these Earther names right?

The important part is to know what's big and bold, and that's this one special building. Sure, no Earther's mastered the pinnacle of architecture, AKA slime-based masonry, but LC von Hessen shows us one hot new design that'll make your head spin in *"Hivemind."*

And when it comes to Earther bodies taking a turn in ways they shouldn't—again, I'm telling you, slime-based is the way to go!—something's a little fishy in that cooler the sorority gals keep dragging around. I'm no expert, but Stephanie Gray will hook you up, all researched there and back on *"The Secret of Theta Pi."*

Of course, getting hooked up isn't always what it's cracked up to be. No, I don't mean the time the Venusians used me as a space fishing lure. I mean all those gizmos and doodads and machines the Earthers love, the kind that show them holograms and music and awful societies. Diana Fenves knows more with *"The Long Sleep."*

What no one should ever sleep on is sweets. Brownies, cookies, and especially cakes. *What?* I'm a *slime of discerning tastes.* Same with the dome-based Earthers hunting for the right ingredients in Sim Kern's trek into trouble, *"Real Sugar Is Hard to Find."*

But then, if you really want to tangle with trouble, Laura Barker tells us all about *"Ma Dresden."* There's a whole rundown in this story of why you don't want to get on Ma Dresden's bad side—maybe not her good side either, not any side! Rocket into space to get away.

And that's where our last story takes place, out in the star ocean, where Earthers can't wait to escape from each other—especially when some of them are walking death-predicting-algae-corpses, stalking people on a starship. Lindsay King-Miller will give you the scoop with *"An Eventual Feast."*

Hang on a tic, everyone. Hailey Piper won't quit banging on the airlock door, so let's activate the little comm box and hear her deal.

What's that? Speak up! You're proud of these authors? Honored to work with Scummy? Of course you are.

That's a silly thing to worry about when you're living in an airlock, but one life lesson I'll share with her, as the computer likes to say each time I steer

TRANSMISSION: SCUMM

our ship into a pleasant asteroid field, *"Shield capacity terminal—kssshh— disabling manual pilot—kssssssshh—AI override activated—kssssshh—alterna- tive route selected."*

Anyway, enough with the sneak peeks and sad stowaways. On with the stories and the good Scumm groove!

SUMMER 2021 | SPARK & FIZZ BOOKS PRESENTS | ISSUE #11

SNAKE EYES

Spark & Fizz Books, 2021
Portland | Boston | Outer Space

SNAKE
EYES

AUTHOR BIOS

ANA GARDNER left her home in the Transylvanian foothills for the windier shores of New England, where she now works as a cognitive scientist and full-time puppy wrangler. In her free time, she writes about anxious badass ladies finding happy endings. Her stories have appeared or are upcoming in *Cast of Wonders*, *Apparition Lit*, *DSF*, and others.

AVERY KIT MALONE is a CR 8, medium sized aberration (chaotic/neutral, if you were wondering). His fiction appears in *Pseudopod*, *Novel Noctule*, and *Dim Shores Presents*, among other venues. You can call to him across the void at @dead_scholar.

LC VON HESSEN is a writer of horror, weird fiction, and general unpleasantness. They have previously appeared in such publications as *Vastarien*, *Nightscript*, and *Beyond the Book of Eibon*. An ex-Midwesterner, von Hessen lives in Brooklyn with a talkative orange cat.

STEPHANIE GRAY is an Aquarius of dubious moral character. She is the author of several odd and cerebral works of fiction including the novella *Lockhart and Teague: the Empty Chest.*

DIANA FENVES is a science fiction writer and playwright. She received her MFA in Fiction at NC State University. She is passionate about confronting the unjust and the uncomfortable through art. She lives in Raleigh with her husband and dog. More at dianafenves.com.

SIM KERN is an environmental journalist and speculative fiction writer living along the Gulf Coast. Their debut novella, *Depart, Depart!* explores intersections of climate change, social justice, and ghosts. You can find links to all their published work at www.simkern.com

LAURA BARKER is a writer, artist, and facilitator. She runs an LGBTQIA+ Black writing group. Her work has appeared in *Apparition Lit*, and *midnight & indigo*, and she is writer in residence for Spread the Word's "This Is Our Place."

LINDSAY KING-MILLER is the author of *Ask a Queer Chick: A Guide to Sex, Love, and Life for Girls who Dig Girls*. Her fiction has appeared in the anthologies *The Fiends in the Furrows*, *Terror at 5280'*, *Tiny Nightmares*, and numerous other publications. She lives in Denver, CO.

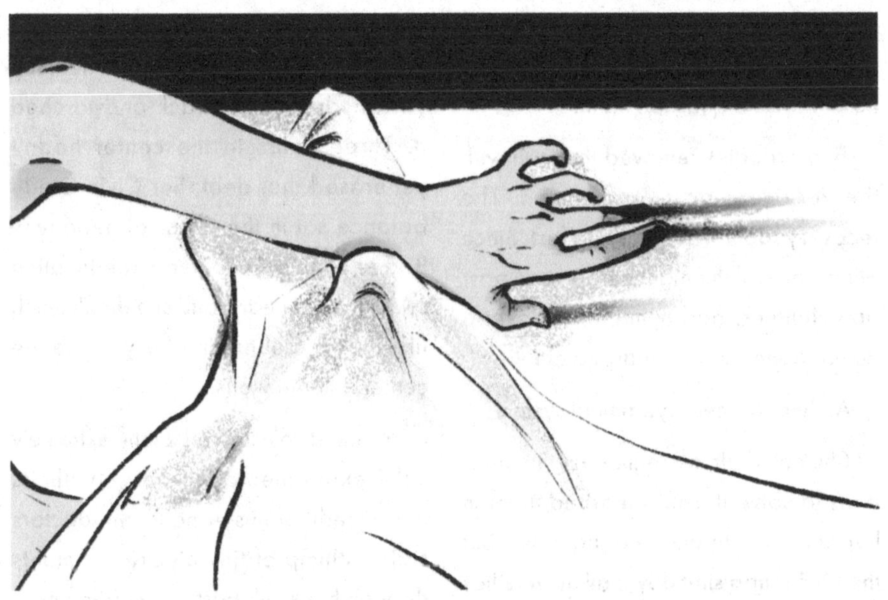

ANA GARDNER

A DEFIANCE OF VIOLINS

Blood trickled from Nina's ear. A normal side effect of the neuroport implant, said the doctors. If she keeled over from an aneurysm, the same doctors would shrug, adjust their protocols, and try the experimental surgery again on someone else, all with the same reassuring smile.

Their *entirely voluntary experimental* surgery. So said the papers Nina had signed, in which she gave the re-education center consent to stick a data port into her brain.

Across the post-op room, a man began convulsing in his cot. After a minute, his choked gasps faded, and his body slumped to the floor. A doctor in sterile slacks pressed the wall buzzer.

"Clean-up crew, please." He smiled hearteningly at the other volunteers. "A very rare post-operatory reaction. This is an extremely safe procedure."

The consent forms said so, too.

Nina wiped her red-stained fingertips on the sheets of her recovery cot.

Kind of the doctors to bother with consent forms at all, really. The Peaceable Order controlled everything from the ash-cloud in the west to the diesel-sludge shores back east; if they chose to drill into Nina's brain with corkscrews, no one would question them.

Two orderlies removed the man with the very rare post-op reaction. The recovery room was emptying fast. Since Nina's arrival the night before, two post-op volunteers had come in and over a dozen gone out via clean-up crew.

An imbalanced dynamical system.

She could almost remember the equations to solve it: she'd learned them in her first college engineering class. But the Order had shut down all universities that year. So she'd taken refuge in the old city junkyard instead, with a stolen gardening toolbox, and discovered she preferred the practical stuff to the fancy math anyway.

Another thud and a bowel whistle flagged a new volunteer expiring. The doctor pressed the wall buzzer again.

"He had a pre-existing condition," he said, though everyone knew volunteers had to be perfectly healthy.

Three years ago, Nina might've argued. Shouted at the doctor, thrown a punch, even. But the center had since been gently reminding her about the Freedom of Orderly Protest Act. The best protest was one expressed *politely*, one that didn't make anyone uncomfortable.

Nina had defied the FOPA once, when Order officers had found her junkyard hydroponics shack and torched it. Three years in the center hadn't yet erased that debt; her Civic Credit balance sat in the abysmal negatives. Bad enough to keep her in reeducation several more years, and she didn't much like the idea of turning forty inside the center's sterile walls.

So she'd volunteered for the extremely safe experimental surgery—with its hefty credit bonus—and let the doctors stab a clump of tiny electric filaments through her skull, past the middle occipital and superior temporal lobes, and into the hippocampus.

And now here she was, neuroport stuck in her head and ears bleeding normally. The clean-up crews stuff the latest volunteer into a body bag.

"Please remember to fill out your hourly symptom report," the doctor said, in his cheery voice. "And don't worry—most violent tremors and severe bleeding should fade quickly!"

Nina lay back down on her cot, and she waited to die.

She lived, and that drove her Civic Credit way up. Suddenly she had her own cell, a comfy six-by-eight with a cot and two working air vents.

A DEFIANCE OF VIOLINS

Doctors came by daily to make her memorize word lists and do squats. She got two food rations a day—real food, too, none of that NutriShake stuff made from bugs and old carcasses. Nina had once sworn to starve before drinking those, but hunger strikes were *disorderly* protest. The shakes tasted like chicken, if you didn't think too hard about it.

For weeks, she enjoyed luxurious space and meals, and all she had to do was not die.

Then the doctor came in with a center technician in blue overalls, carrying wires and an electric box. They stuck a cord into Nina's port and walked her around the halls for an hour, then the doctor sat her down, pulled a chip from the electric box, and plugged it into her port.

Nina's head split down the middle.

One eye still saw her cell. One ear heard screams, and one hand clawed at the air. But her other eye saw the corridor she'd walked on, and the tips of her black socks. Though she lay still, half her body felt the sway of walking, and the weight of footsteps thumped against her left foot.

"Lateralization", the doctors called it, later. Her port had been implanted a little too far right, which prevented an *immersive experience*.

They fixed implant protocols, and no one else suffered the same problem. After Nina, the neuroport surgery succeeded every time.

'New Entertainment!' all public screens soon said. 'Peaceable, Order-approved immersive experiences. Coming soon to every Residence-Block shop!'

To earn the rest of her Civic Credit balance, Nina volunteered to test the new entertainment chips. After all, if they worked on her *lateralized* port, they'd work on anyone.

Each afternoon, the same tech in blue overalls led her to a small testing room with insulated walls, sat her in a metal chair, and connected a chip-reader/writer machine to her port.

"I'm inserting the experience chip now," she warned Nina every time, in a flat, quiet voice. "On the count of three."

The chips fractured Nina's world into strange, splintered bits. Often, she was so nauseous and disoriented she could barely answer the testing questions. She needed breaks and a puking bucket, and she swore enough to earn several orderly protest violation notices. But slowly, things improved.

Maybe her brain adjusted, or center engineers made better chips based on her feedback. The nausea faded, her focus sharpened.

After a month, she could process the chip-trip and the testing room at the same time and switch between them easily.

"Immersive rating? Please use a zero-to-ten scale."

The tech always asked the same questions, in the exact same order.

"Ten. Authenticity rating... four. Corn fields usually smell like dust and dry stalks, not whatever this flowery smell is. And they're usually quieter. Think more mice than songbirds."

The tech's eyes met hers, briefly, with a hint of curiosity quickly masked.

A DEFIANCE OF VIOLINS

"I grew up in the foothills of Caribou Mountain. South of the Kennebec," said Nina. "Cornfields in every backyard." She smirked. "I didn't realize how well I remembered them."

The tech held her eyes for a moment, then lowered her gaze back to the survey pad.

"Please stay on task," she murmured. "Have you experienced any of the following side effects..."

Nina shrugged and fell back into describing the usual tingling in her skull that made her teeth itch.

She didn't take the rebuff personally. The center didn't allow small talk. Though the room was shielded so outside electric signals wouldn't interfere with testing, officers could probably listen in. She didn't need more violation notices on her barely improved Civic Credit.

She tested more chips, after 'Stare at a Cornfield.' First basic ones, like 'Hold a Rose' or 'Watch the Clear Night Sky.' Then the center developed a higher-end line—'Walk Through a Warm Bakery,' 'Climb an Apple Tree,' 'Run Barefoot on a Sunny Beach.' Somehow, each chip reminded Nina of the old house in the foothills, of summers running in the apple orchards or the damp, noisy woods, and biking up cracked asphalt between goat pastures.

She'd not seen pastures in twenty years. The Order kept some viable land, but she'd long given up on the idea of finding it. She'd adjusted to the dust clouds and drought winds and the concrete flood-safe city blocks, and had left old memories to fade, like the dynamical system equations she'd never finished learning.

But the center's chip-trips plucked the memories back up, one by one—and with them, old thoughts Nina hadn't made room for since she'd fled her closed-down college campus.

"Any other side effects to report?" As always, the tech ran through the survey in a flat business voice. "Please include anything not covered by the standard questions."

"Nothing," said Nina.

The center didn't need to know how climbing apple trees made her think of a time before the Order. Or how each chip helped her focus, made her pay more attention.

Made her care.

The tech tapped the stylus to the pad, then lowered it. Curiosity filled her eyes again; only this time, instead of looking away, she reached for the chip-reader/writer on the table and turned a knob all the way to the left. A high-pitched noise filled the room, making Nina wince.

"Why do you stay?" the tech asked, so softly Nina had to guess the shape of the words on her lips. "You've enough credit by now for a job in a Resi-Block. Even if it's a low-tier one..."

She didn't add 'it's better than this,' but Nina understood.

"You stayed, too." They'd never spoken before the chip-trip tests, but she had a good memory for faces. "You were a resident when I first came. Now you work for them."

The tech shrugged. "Safe job. Good way to build credit."

But her bruised eyes flickered to the door, and Nina again understood: she didn't have enough credit to leave, yet. She wondered what this woman had done to earn a civic debt larger than her own.

The shrill noise faded. As the tech reached and turned the knob back, Nina noticed an old scaly patch on her collarbone, like a smattering of old, healed pockmark scars. Then the tech straightened, and the blue fabric obscured the old scar.

"Recording feedback," she explained in her usual, flat tone. "It shouldn't transmit to your neuroport, but if you feel any tingling or experience ear pain, please report it."

Nina nodded, but when their eyes met again, she smiled. In the dim testing room, among padded walls lit only by two pinhole lamps, a silent smile seemed an acceptable risk.

The tech nodded back, mouth twisting fleetingly before she focused on unwiring the chip-reader. From her motions, less choppy and rushed than usual, and the looser slant of her shoulders, Nina thought she seemed... pleased.

How strange, to understand so much meaning from so much silence. Nina had never been a people person. She'd preferred living alone in her junkyard shack, with only her peas and carrots and zucchini in tin cans full of dirt for company. At the center, she'd spoken only when she had to, and never wished to know anyone better.

Until now.

Perhaps the chip-trips had changed her brain more than she'd realized. Made her want things she'd never wanted before. Smiles. Companionship.

Or maybe she'd wanted them once—when she was a schoolgirl and the Order barely a side mention in newspaper columns—and she'd forgotten.

Next testing session, Nina tapped the chip-reader and gave the tech a curious look. The tech nodded and unwired the box more slowly, pausing so Nina

A DEFIANCE OF VIOLINS

could see where each wire went and read the labels on the little sockets.

When she paused, the fingers of her left hand tapped a jerky rhythm on the metal box. Her ring and index fingers always struck the same two spots, Nina noticed—like they moved in a choreographed dance. The tech saw her looking and snapped her fingers to draw her attention. Nina grinned.

It was a silent little teaching, all their own. They said little with words, much with their faces. Nina discovered what her eyes could say, her eyebrows, a wrinkle of her nose and the corners of her lips.

Despite the headaches, testing hour became the best part of her days. The center didn't use names—the tech's blue overalls had no name label, and Nina's tan shirt showed only her resident number, a string of digits she tried not to memorize. But Nina privately named the tech May. That had been her favorite month, once, back when weather still changed season to season and she could see apple trees with her whole brain, not just the neuroport hull.

She itched to ask for May's true name. Give her own. But *unauthorized information exchange* was a worse offense than swearing, and neither of them could afford the credit fine.

She never learned what landed May in reeducation, either. She tried to guess, and asked with her eyes. But May only returned a slight smile, hooded eyes crinkling at the corners.

Only months later, at the end of a testing session, did May abruptly turn the knob on the chip-reader all the way to the left again. The machine gave a shrill whine—but before Nina could ask all the questions she'd been saving, May put a hand atop hers.

"You need to go." Her voice was rushed, breathless. "They're bringing new chips to test. Tell them you're done, and leave before the new chips arrive."

"Why?" asked Nina, stupidly. But the feedback noise died before May could answer.

It didn't matter. A week later, Nina understood the warning, when May, pale and tense, brought in a chip marked *'Enforcement,'* rather than the usual *'Entertainment.'*

The Order had thought to use chip-trips as punishment, too. Their latest batch, rather than *'Ride a Horse'* or *'Touch a Sunflower,'* was *'Twenty Zap-Rod Strikes at Medium Voltage.'*

Nina respectfully put in her request to leave the center after that. It was approved within the customary twelve weeks, and her civic-credit updated to reflect her good work. She departed in an orderly manner, fully reeducated, and with seven testing chips hidden in the sleeve of her overalls. Those, May had slipped to her in their last session, with one of her fleeting smiles.

She couldn't tell May goodbye. But she carried the touch of their hands, the warmth of May's dry, scarred fingertips, in the same place she carried the memory of apple trees in the rain.

Nina got a job scrubbing smog filters at Resi-Block 18, a fifteen-hour shift with one hour for lunch and necessities. Not a bad deal. The other jobs her Civic Credit allowed were diesel-sludge shore scavenging, with triple the mortality rate, old metal reclamation, and sewage maintenance. She preferred climbing thirty-foot smog-collectors to handling the city's refuse.

She shared a shift-bed with two other scrubbers and sold chip-trips on the side for extra rations. At the end of each week, she sold the rations for extra resi-credit, until she could afford her own bed full time. She rented out the bed during her work-hours, until she could afford a semiprivate: a cot surrounded by blackout curtains.

That night, five months after leaving the reeducation center, Nina pulled shut the gray cloth curtains and inventoried the contents of her hidden pockets.

Aside from the seven Center chips, she'd collected five basic ones delivered to Resi-Block shops. She'd traded around for a chip-reader/writer and a tinkering kit, and wires, bolts, and other scraps she'd scavenged on the job.

Rewiring neurochips wasn't easy. But Nina was a clever tinkerer—even in school, before the Order, she'd always been winning science fairs with green bioware and renewable batteries that everyone praised and no one used. And May's silent teaching had given her a head start.

She plugged in two chips and crossed then re-crossed the wires, testing the results on herself. She suffered weeks of headaches, half-immersed in fractured experiences, but in the end, from 'Picking Berries' and 'Watching the Rain,' she made a new chip: 'Picking Berries in the Rain.'

Later, she made 'Eating Apples in a Sunny Park' and 'Smelling Flowers in the Rain.' Delicious mixed sensations that even high-end chips, available only at the Order Store, couldn't provide.

She kept one chip to herself, hidden in her sleeve—but all others, she shared.

People came to trade. Food, blankets, cola pop. Even those from the fancier

A DEFIANCE OF VIOLINS

Resi-Blocks, with glass-roofed atria and indoor vegetable patches, and no permanent filter-motors thrumming in their walls, liked Nina's custom chip-trips. They offered her sunscreen or dried seeds and soil, and they wanted special-request chips.

But Nina already had her own plan for special requests. She began asking neighbors—those who dared answer—what memories they missed from before the Order.

'Country Fair' took her a month to make from 'Eating Apples' and 'Walking in a Meadow on Summer Nights' and 'Smelling Fried Dough.' For 'Bike Ride,' she ended up building a dingy bicycle and riding it downhill on a particularly cloudy night, clutching the chip recorder, the exhilaration of speed and motion, complemented nicely by her fear of getting caught. 'Sailing' she couldn't get right, but she came close with 'Sea Breeze' and a rocking chair of her own design. May would be proud, she thought.

She gave away the new custom chips for free.

"Take them and test them," she told the neighbors, "and tell me if I got them right."

They took the chips, and later came back to tell her of country fair songs and their favorite fried foods. Of riding bikes not on roads, but in damp forests full of wild strawberries. Their eyes lit up as they spoke, and they began passing her custom chips between them and arguing with each other about funnel cake and the best town for lobster rolls.

More neighbors came forward to tell her what they missed. Tomato gardens. Halloween parades. Scotch. Nina mixed every chip she could, into approximations of their lost memories.

One day, a gray-haired man with sunken eyes stopped by just before lights-out and said, in a voice quiet as thought: "Disorderly protest."

Nina held his gaze, and they smiled in the sudden, loud silence.

"I had a daughter," he said. "She liked to build things, too. Told her to come home when they closed the schools, but she wouldn't. She signed the objector act and stayed on campus."

Nina knew of the campus objectors—students and faculty who'd defied the shutdown orders. The Order forces had crushed them within weeks.

The old man pulled from his pocket a chip too big to fit neuroports. An old data drive. He put it into Nina's hand.

"She played the violin. Not as good as this—but this is all I could find. I wanted you to have it. Make it into one of your chips and let others hear it, too."

Nina nodded. The old man smiled, thumbed his nose at her, and he left.

Next morning, he was in the court-yard at sun-up, protesting the Order. He carried a handwritten sign that read 'Fuck FOPA.' Nina rushed outside, her chip-writer in the pockets of her scrubbing overalls, and she recorded herself watching him, until officers rushed in with zap-rods.

The man ran toward the mess of trash compactors and filter equipment in the backyard. Nina hoped he'd outrun them. Unlikely—but she hoped, anyway.

She left the new chip unlabeled and didn't share it as she did all others. For many days, she worked only on transferring the contents of the old man's data drive into a chip her neuroport could read. When done at last, she plugged the translated chip into her port. A small stage, brightly lit, appeared before her left eye, and a young man in a black suit.

The image was grainy and tremulous, not made for the neuroport interface. Static pricked Nina's neck as the man bowed, then tucked a violin between his left cheek and his shoulder.

The sound was tremulous, too; the neuroport-translated audio came in uneven, stuttering waves. Yet the longer she listened, the easier it became to focus on the melody underneath the noise. The man moved as he played, turning his upper body to the music, sinking and rising with the long, penetrant notes. His motions carried Nina through the piece just as the violin did, until her room vanished and the constant thrum of filters shaking the walls faded from focus, and all that was left was the stage and the young man and his song.

The first immersive experience her lateralized neuroport had ever allowed. And it came from a clunky old data drive, and a long-gone musician playing a piece she'd never heard of.

On a particularly deep turn, as he cut a long note on the strings, she noticed a red, scaly patch on his collarbone. Just like May's, only angrier. Fresher.

Nina smiled.

A violin rash. May had once been a violinist. It made sense. Artists had been the first rounded into reeducation. She'd never thought May, with her flat, business-like voice and the jerky taps of her fingers on the chip-reader, a musician. But it felt right.

Nina listened through to the end, thinking of May.

She then took out the unlabeled chip of the old man condemning the Order, and she spent the night mixing the two, pounding head bobbing to the stuttering violin in her left ear. She'd never known for sure why May had smuggled her those seven chips, back at the center. But she thought it was for something like this.

Nina offered the chip to the next neighbor who came to trade, and told him to pass it on.

"It's called 'Disorderly Protest'," she said, and the neighbor frowned and nodded, silent. Nina didn't know if he did pass it on—but a week later, walking back to her room, she thought she heard a low whistle in a familiar, rising and sinking melody.

When officers showed up at her door with one of her rewired chips, she wasn't all that surprised. The Order always found out, eventually.

"Unauthorized initiative," spat one of the officers, pulling the zap-rod from its holster.

It was an innocuous chip—Nina's oldest, 'Picking Berries in the Rain.'

It didn't violate FOPA. But for someone in her Civic Credit range, any offense was grounds for Justice Court.

As officers dragged her away, her Resi-Block 18 neighbors looked away, looked down. Yet some, before they did, risked holding her gaze. Their silence filled the barren courtyard.

Nina was judged summarily, in a near-empty room. She wasn't important enough to broadcast her trial to Resi-Block public screens; the hovercams by the ceiling were turned off.

"Guilty," said the judge, and she shrugged. Everyone in Justice Court was guilty.

Her sentence—working recycling at the Nutrishake factory—was a standard punishment for those who repeatedly broke the peace.

"I only reminded people what they were missing," she said, stumbling as an Order officer shoved her to the side-door marked SENTENCED. "It'll take someone else to make them do anything about it."

That was the trick, she'd figured. May had taught her to use chip-writers and given her the testing chips. Nina had used them to remind people of a time before the Order. Someone else could take It from there.

The officer snarled and struck her with his zap-rod, and he pushed her out into a long, grey-walled corridor. At the far end, a rusted door led to a dim cement tunnel which linked the Justice Court to the Nutrishake factory.

The tunnel must've once been a sewage route: the long drought had dried its contents to desiccated gunk and sealed in decades-old rank odors.

Nina watched the walls, searching for the rusted grates that had once led to sewer pipes. Once she spotted one, she let her eyes wander to the officer's stern profile. A neuroport sat under his cropped yellow hair. She wondered if he knew she'd been the first to survive that surgery.

His was a perfect port, not lateralized, like hers. *Full immersive experience.*

Nina slowed, pointing up with a cuffed hand. "What's that bird doing in here?"

As he turned his head, she slipped the chip from her own neuroport and, in one smooth move, plugged it into his. The officer crashed to the floor, convulsing.

"*Twenty Zap-Rod Strikes, at Medium Voltage,*" Nina explained. "The oldest Enforcement chip prototype. It's a little miscalibrated for pain levels—I heard they fixed that, in later models."

The officer's truncated screams bounced along the sludge-caked walls. But only sentenced prisoners ever walked the grim, dank tunnel. He quit screaming, at last, and stilled. Nina stared down at him.

"He had a pre-existing condition," she murmured, thoughtfully.

She bent to retrieve the chip. Then, taking the officer's zap-rod and coat, she walked back to the rusted grate that was a leftover from the old sewage system.

The rod helped budge the old iron from its place, and Nina slipped into the hot, rank pipe. There was nowhere to go, but she dragged forward, anyway. On a turn, she dislodged another gunk crusted grate and slipped into another tunnel, dark save for the glowing tip of her zap-rod. She wandered the winding, long-abandoned conduits, going largely by her nose, hoping the least-odorous routes might exit back to the surface.

As she stumbled into ever-older and narrower pipes, odd echoes bounced about her, muffled in the thick silence. A hiss rang out nearby, soft and uneven, like a draft of wind. But the silence changed, after the hiss, and Nina knew it hadn't been the wind.

She thought of May, who'd taught her the language of the wordless.

"I'm not Order," she said, and as the echo of her words faded, the silence changed again.

Nina had never been good at whistling but she tried, in the dark, to whistle the violin's tune. It sounded so horribly mangled, to her ears, it nearly made her laugh.

"I'm just looking for a way out," she said. "No trouble."

     A DEFIANCE OF VIOLINS

More silence. Then, a rough voice said, "Drop the rod."

Nina did, leaning it tip-up against the wall and backing away. The gleam of its cold, white light showed the silhouettes peeling from the shadows, walking toward her.

One came before the others—a tall, broad-shouldered woman, who stopped and picked up the zap-rod, aiming it at Nina like a flashlight.

"Childhood impressions," she said, in the same gravelly voice that had told Nina to drop the rod.

Nina frowned. "What?"

"The violin song. Enescu's *Childhood Impressions*. Half of the first piece, to be precise. Called *The Wandering Fiddler*."

Nina squinted, blinking against the zap-rod's glow. "Is there something I don't know about violin lovers and defying the Order?"

The woman laughed and lowered the rod. Behind her, someone clicked on a proper lamp, sending flickering copper shadows dancing on the gunk-encrusted walls. The woman was older, Nina saw, with deep crow's feet at the corner of her dark eyes.

"How do you know that song, then," she asked Nina, "but you don't know its name?"

Her tone made plain she already knew the answer. But Nina said anyway, "Heard it on a mixed chip."

"And what did you think of the chip?"

Nina bit back a smile. The question reminded her of May's testing surveys.

The others' silence had taken on an expectant quality, tinged with tension.

"I used to think I'd go back to gardening, after reeducation," she said. "Scrub filters 'til I qualified for the arthropod nursery, then make cricket bars a few years to work my way up to the greenhouses. Nice, quiet job. But one of you fiddler types got in my way." Nina smiled. "So now I think I'd like to find her, if I can. See if she wants to do some unauthorized gardening together."

It surprised her to say the words out loud. She'd never let herself dwell on it—but every time she asked a neighbor what they missed, she pictured May, and their quiet hours in the dim testing room. Jarring headaches and refuse bucket and all.

"So that's what I was thinking of, with that chip," she finished. "And I could use help. If you're looking for a high-risk, disorderly sort of enterprise."

The woman smiled crookedly, the lines around one corner of her mouth deepening.

She asked Nina, "Do you know what a group of violinists call themselves?"

Nina shrugged. "Old music's not really my thing. An orchestra? A string quartet?"

"I can tell it's not your thing," snorted the woman.

She turned off the zap-rod and vanished it up the long sleeve of her coat, waving Nina along. "Come and tell me about this disorderly fiddler of yours. We're always looking for new players."

Nina smiled and followed her into the dark.

AVERY KIT MALONE

THE HOLLOW STARS IN HEAVEN

In the dirty red-green neon glow and sea of laughter and voices amplified by drunkenness, I seethe through the crowds and sip my whiskey. It's a Saturday night and my skin is restless.

Restless enough to draw me in to old places, old habits. In this bar, it's dim enough that I almost feel safe. Almost expect that no one can decipher more of me than an indistinct shadow hovering beyond the periphery of any group.

It doesn't take me long to realize this was a mistake. I see, too late, a member of the old crew—washed-out men I haunted this and other venues with—

and one head turns, then two, faces scrunched in concentration. They are looking at my face, eyes like paring knives, peeling away layers to look for what they might recognize underneath. Those eyes flash with recognition—not of me, but me in a past life—and I turn away sharply. Before I can see their faces crease with disgust. Before I might hear them calling at my back.

I'm too tired for this shit.

I stumble through to the farthest, darkest corner, and it's a bit quieter here. I don't stop until a throng of people separates us, and I know the group's eyes like knives in my back are only imagined. Wanting some connection with someone, something to keep them at bay, I turn to the man leaning against the wall beside me and give a whiskey-emboldened grin.

In the dark, I see a gaunt frame, tall. Black button-down, belt and slacks clinging to his thin frame like a half-discarded shed. The glass in his hand is cold and clear and could be anything. His eyes are bold in the dim light, embers in darkened pits, and the shine to them—something bright and fervent there, and I wonder if he might be rolling. His head is utterly shaved and I hesitate, wondering if I'm dealing with a skinhead, but no—doesn't have that vibe about him. Instead, he simply seems... off. But he smiles back.

"I'm Leo," I say, extending my hand.

He stares at it, apparently hesitating. Well, shit. Probably straight. Wandered in for a drink, not knowing.

But then he grasps my hand, an oddly mechanical motion that slides into gentleness; he holds my hand for just that much longer than he should. He doesn't offer his name. Instead, he says, "Here... with others?"

"Just me this time around."

We have some bullshit conversation, though he seems earnestly engaged in our small talk. Too measured, coherent, to be ecstasy or anything else I know, I decide. Possibly he is just insane.

We end up in a stall in the men's room. In the cold light, I can see him a bit more clearly. He is passive but eager. I am happy to oblige, happier yet when he doesn't turn on me. No revulsion. Not even a hint of surprise at what I am.

"Let's head to my place," I hear myself saying.

"Your place," he echoes in agreement.

If the drab confines of my tiny, shitty apartment in any way defy his expectations, he doesn't show it.

Instead, in my bedroom, I am surprised as I peel away his shirt button by button, by the intricate system of symbols, runes, and circles and lines arranged in tattoos spanning his body, so carefully designed they surely bear some esoteric meaning. He doesn't comment on them. I don't bother to ask.

In the quiet darkness of my room, he is not passive. He moves with hunger and frenetic obsession. It is outside of anything I have experienced.

I am happy to oblige.

I invite him inside many times after that. He appears at my doorstep. I don't know his name and it feels unimportant.

THE HOLLOW STARS IN HEAVEN

I often find him staring out the window up at the sky, sometimes craning his entire neck to fit his face through the lifted mesh like a highway-bound dog, and peering up with something unreadable but seemingly heartfelt at the lid of clouds and light over the city that masks the stars beyond. Sometimes I hear him laugh quietly, facing the ceiling, or in a dark corner alone.

One night, I am doing something parallel to sleep, sweating and restless in the bed as I am prone to be. He is breathing evenly beside me, his eyes wide open in what might—or might not—be actual sleep. My phone begins to buzz on the table beside me and, exhaustion-drugged, I slide it over and answer it without checking.

It's been so long that I've gotten complacent.

"Livvy," says a voice hoarse with emotion—or perhaps from fervent prayer late into the night—breathless in a rush to speak before I can respond, "I want you to know I've been praying for you. When you decide to live a normal life, you always have a place he—"

I've cut the call and slammed my phone down before my mind has fully caught up with me. He's shifting around behind me. I roll around to find the gleam of his eyes, that febrile light in the dark.

"They think my life is a sin," I say.

"*Sin.*" He tests the word with his mouth.

I don't know if it's his quirk of echolalia or a question, but I decide to keep talking.

"They always held heaven over my head like a cinderblock. Can't get in with a life of sin."

He startles me with a burst of laughter. I look at his face and see only those impossible eyes, vivid like a snake's, like a cat's in the dark—but no light shines for them to reflect.

"There is no *sin* or absence of *sin* in heaven. Heaven is a dead place. It's full of ghosts."

He is still laughing, quietly, when I somehow fall asleep. I dream of a field of unbroken darkness, impossible pressure; something coiled around me, pulsating. A single distant point of light opening like an eye.

The solitude and dark like a blanket. The blinding light, a dagger.

The needle glides out of my skin and leaves a bead of irritable red welling on my thigh. I'm patching it over with a bandage while he watches in quiet fascination from several feet away.

"Your name," I say.

He says something bizarre.

I snap my head up. He has a way of looking calm and feverishly, deliriously happy at once. He repeats himself, a string of syllables I can't follow. Something sounding like it should require two throats at once.

"My name," he clarifies.

"Well, do you have, like, a nickname?" I say.

He's swaying back and forth as if to music I can't hear, ever so gently, and my internal pendulum of categorizing him swings back to *drugs*.

"And what do you do?" I prompt him further, lying back on my bed and watching his unfathomable smile. "Where are you from?"

"I'm a... *ghost*. Ancient *ghost*. I came here from inside a sun-star-corpse, distant."

The pendulum swings again. Madman, it is.

"A star ghost," I say.

"Yes. Sleeping in cores of stars and planets. Vast dreamers, dreaming vast dreams."

"Gods?" I offer. "Sounds more like gods to me." He doesn't seem to understand the difference.

"Okay, let's go back to the planets," I say. "How about Earth? Earth has a ghost living inside of it?"

"Yes," he says. "It hates you all."

I'd believe it.

"Okay," I say. I'm starting to feel a headache coming on, and I'm wishing he would leave now. I debate kicking him out. He doesn't seem the violent type; he'd probably comply. "So you're an alien god-ghost. What were you doing in the gay bar on Market Street?"

"Wandering... Heard the sound. Voices. Sea of voices. Felt familiar. I wanted to drown in it," he says.

"Prove it," I say abruptly.

"Prove it?" he echoes.

"Prove you're not human," I say.

"Okay," he says.

Something goes wrong with his eyes, right at once. They start to shake and slide askew; something black starts to rim them as though he's crying tar, and it slides down his cheeks with the consistency of semi-congealed blood. He opens his mouth, making a sound like someone coughing *inward*, a gasping sort of choking sound. A dark thing begins to squirm its way up from the shadowed depths of his throat, black and gleaming, and the tip of it writhes out of his mouth—

"Get out," I yell, standing.

He startles back into himself. Looks at me blankly.

THE HOLLOW STARS IN HEAVEN

"Get out. Get the *fuck out!*"

He pauses and I sense hesitation. An unknowable chain of thought behind his gleaming eyes—I think of a mantis, or an octopus, his steady, unreadable gaze judging me a threat or not.

And, too, all at once, I see my tone and posture as if in third person, and I see in myself something horrible and mirrored here in too many encounters I've had myself.

The fear and revulsion is clear in my face.

I squeeze my eyes shut. Slow my breath. Say, "Wait."

He tells me he is extremely young, relative to others, as we walk along the riverside, city lights bits of splintered gold on the water. That his star is not yet dead.

That it gets harder to come back, the longer they sleep up there.

He tells me that all the ghosts nestled in the cores of the cooling, luminous corpses of supernovae are waiting.

Dreaming gods, dead but not. The endless dark of space is haunted.

Something is wrong with him. It's evident as soon as he comes over.

He's sluggish, sometimes pausing to steady himself, groaning as one might with a migraine or on the verge of vomiting. Sometimes, he does vomit—a substance like bloody tar, with fat granules of what looks like coal interspersed within. I watch with distaste as it bubbles on my bathroom tile.

"What is going on with you?" I finally ask him.

One eye swivels to me, but he appears to have lost the fight for the other; it rolls shakily up into his eyelid.

"Losing tether," he says through a stiffened jaw. "Must go home soon."

I consider this. He stumbles to my front door.

"Where are you going?" I say. It's nearing midnight.

"Fan club," he says, a lunatic smile flashing at me from over his shoulder. "Church."

I follow.

In the shambling ruin of what was once a warehouse by the river, a surprising coterie awaits, unbothered by the thick dust that flashes like stars beneath dour industrial ceiling lights.

Many are well-dressed. Some are cloaked in filthy rags. They all glare at me as I enter, tight faced and quiet

when I pass; a ripple of murmurs trails in my wake. Whether their dislike is born of the fact that I'm an outsider to their esoteric enclave or because I fucked their god for three weeks remains to be seen.

I've dealt with far more cutting hatred, though, and I take my seat in a front-row chair. The dilapidated building is empty aside from this make-shift nave. The concrete floors are stained and damp; the walls, rust-mottled metal sheets.

My companion drags himself to the front, to the pulpit made of a podium and a microphone wired to speakers on either side. He steadies himself by gripping it with white knuckles. I am immediately forgotten by everyone else, and all eyes attune to him.

In a rambling speech replete with odd lexical choices and his idiosyncratic prosody, I gather that he is "wearing their priest" as a "sacrifice-gift," and that his brief visit is at its end. That he must go back to sleep. Back home.

He's chosen the person to take back with him. The crowd's anticipation is thick in the air. You could hear a mouse pissing in the rafters in the breathless vacuum.

His speech ends; his eyes refuse to steady, and so his entire head lolls toward me.

And, oh, their glares are *lethal* all around.

"Come home?" he says.

I stand and go to the front, along with a matronly woman whose style and bearing reek of suburbia, complete with polite condescension.

He collapses before I get there, trembling in a violent seizure, black foam pooling at his mouth. And then something black and gleaming pulls itself from his mouth, long and ropy, coiling and uncoiling spastically, and hovers above—a dark, impossible shape with a sunbright glow emanating from its deepest center.

I look down at the "priest," unmoving in a small puddle of blood and tar, and wonder if he's dead. Then I look again to the thing hovering above.

"What are you waiting for up there?" I ask. "All of you sleeping in stars, waiting. For what?"

New era. Era for us, it says. *Everything will burn and we'll come back.*

I've made my decision. The smirking woman standing beside me hands over a strange, gleaming blade. She shows me the motion I need to make, the odd shape to carve on my flesh. She seems to think the knife's cold edge will scare me off.

Now I smile, staring her in the face. Needles, blade. I'm used to the ritual of opening my skin.

I immediately feel a strange gravity inside of me, a pull in my very guts, and I hear the *clang* of the blade as it clatters to the ground, and I am whirling upward, up beyond the ceiling, with the impossible shape of this alien god above me. I see—or sense—the earth falling away.

The soft blue rim of the atmosphere coalesces below me, encircled by the true dark, and just as soon fades, a marble shrinking into oblivion, and I am moving on and on, at a speed and distance I can't begin to judge.

A sun approaches: young and mind-shatteringly bright. I want to hesitate, but there is no longer a choice. My companion pulls me into it, and the heat sears away my flesh, my being, a sudden wall of agony. My body vaporizes in the heat, bones like charcoal and then crumbling dust and then nothing, insignificant and swallowed like a thimbleful of salt into the hungry sea. And something in me crawls out like a cicada from its feeble husk, onward into the sun.

And I am free. I am purely me, rid of my body and its rituals and needs, all of the pain, both of my lives, my supposed sins. I am essence. A shifting, nebulous body with a core of blinding fire.

Nestled nearby, my companion in our star draws back into itself and gently submerges into its dreams. Scattered around us in the void: other stars like translucent shells to my new eyes, other dreaming ghosts as shadows inside of them, the young suns and the dead and cooling alike. My brothers and sisters. Our scattered brood spans the galaxy.

The heavens are utterly silent. My vision stretches for vast expanses, and I look back for that familiar marble.

Time passes in a new way. In the heart of a star, I rest.

I'm a judge in heaven now. Humanity's absolution will come in a flash of flame. My companion and I, all our ever-patient siblings, we'll descend as a hundred thousand falling stars and live new and radiant lives in the smoldering ash. Free of guilt and suffering. Free from any hiding.

Resplendent lives.

With a vengeful eye turned Earthward, I wait for the coming of a new era.

THE HOLLOW STARS IN HEAVEN

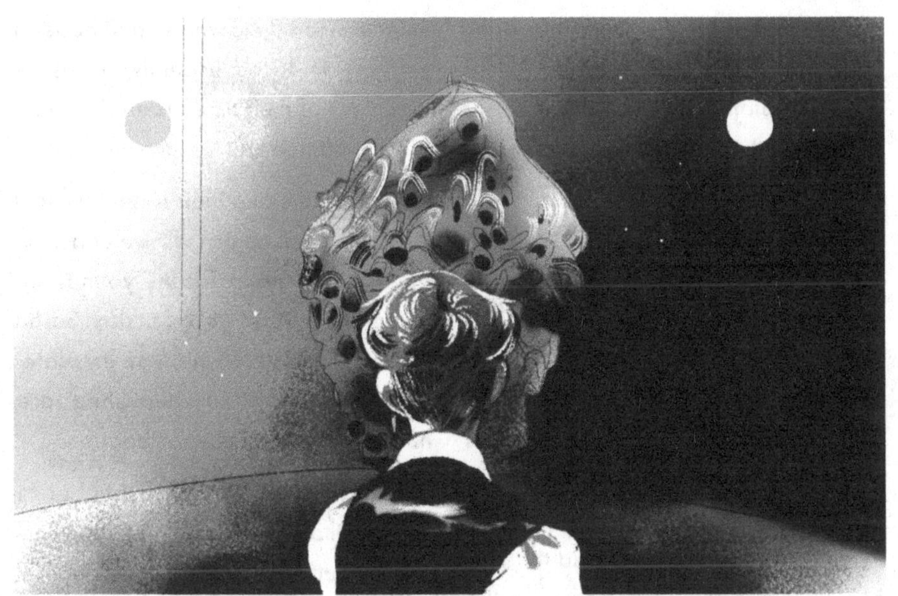

HIVEMIND

They came from every corner of the world, clogging the arteries of public transit, sandals and suitcases sodden with a fresh layer of New York grime.

They came by land, by air, by satellite signal. They came for the Hive, for the Hive was Manhattan's latest, greatest architectural wonder. Part sculpture, part landmark, part Experience, the Hive's multi-story metal bulk was perched at the western rim of the city on a swath of luxury real estate carved out from the former Fisk Park and West Vanderbilt Yard, from the battered corpses of warehouses, tenements, and factories at least a century old, all knocked down and paved over and rebranded as Guilford Gardens before the fine dust of lead and asbestos had settled in the air.

Sasha Lefkovich passed the Hive twice daily on her work commute. Its appeal was utterly foreign to her. The collateral damage alone was bad enough—not so long ago, the worst obstacle in her path from the subway to the office was the plodding gait of fellow commuters whose faces were unnecessarily glued to their phones as they walked, an irritating caricature of 21st-century screen addiction.

Now she routinely found her brisk, confident stride obstructed by tourist couples holding hands in the street or families with confused faces hovering before the subway turnstile or squirming children blocking the escalator's unofficial left-hand express lane, all newly minted Hive pilgrims who didn't understand the accurate pace of working life in Manhattan.

Nor could she fully escape indoors at her desk, as noise pollution from the perpetual construction site that was Guilford Gardens leaked through her office window at all hours like the revolving-door party of an inconsiderate neighbor: a percussive *ratatatatat*, the occasional bleat of an air horn, a low-pitched subterranean rumble that vibrated through her stomach, and most grating of all, a sustained, oddly resonant, high-pitched hum trepanning through her frontal lobe and guiding her hand to the bottle of aspirin in her desk drawer.

For a full year, Sasha had emerged from the subway to face the familiar looming figure of Scabby the Scab-Shaming Rat, an inflatable cartoon grotesque with beady red eyes and a raw-scraped belly covered in dripping pustules. Scabby held court on the sidewalk through heat and snow over a swarm of orange-vested, hard-hatted union men on strike who sipped bodega coffee, grim-faced, under the sun as the machines of their trade roared around them indifferently.

The strikers and their rodent mascot vanished for good on the Hive's opening night launch party for the young, hip, and monied. After work that day, Sasha had descended the subway escalator through a sea of sun-burnished foreheads and Vuitton checkerboard.

The Hive was the brainchild of architect Hamilton Chesebrough VI—24 years old and better known to a certain swath of the internet by his social media handle, @hamncheesebruh6669. He was often caught mugging for the camera, tongue out, horns up, shirt unbuttoned almost to the navel to reveal hints of questionable tattoos, whether on the red carpet or the steps of Machu Picchu. His main pastime was posting talking-head video clips of himself waxing philosophical about ancient aliens or hawking pricey jars of artisanal CBD-infused honey, harvested from his family estate in the Hamptons.

"I fell in love with, like, honeycombs and dodecahedrons," he'd said in a recent podcast interview, pausing to scratch the studied layer of scruff across his neck and jawline. "I just thought it would be a real game-changer to, like, disrupt the landscape, y'know?"

The audio recording popped as he loudly smacked a wad of gum tucked into his cheek.

Hamilton Chesebrough VI had disappeared without warning before the opening night party. Not even his mother or grandfather on the Guilford Gardens board of trustees knew his whereabouts. Most assumed he'd taken yet another impromptu jaunt out to some ancient ruin overseas, a perpetual tourist in his own right.

And so, every day, they came for the Hive. Standing in place, necks craned upward, slack-jawed at the sight. Sasha would see them posing before it with forced grins and roll her eyes, as if on cue.

What was the Hive, exactly?

A hollow, tapering tower of interlinking pathways that coiled around and atop one another to form wide almond-shaped niches through which one could peer outside. These niches were covered with convex panels of plexiglass to discourage picturesque suicides and attendant lawsuits. At dusk, inset lights clicked on to cast a glow throughout each curved pane, shifting from hot pink to neon blue like lasers in the backdrop of a school photo from the year Sasha was born.

The goal of a Hive guest was to ascend the crisscrossing staircases all the way up to the top and take a trophy selfie, enjoying the picturesque view of surrounding skyscrapers like Tammany Tower (the latest residential building for transplanted Manhattanites with a ghastly degree of wealth) and the luxe new Robert Moses Mall (which its social media marketing team was desperately trying to brand as #TheMoze), both of which dwarfed its height considerably, or else gazing out over the New Jersey coastline across the Hudson.

To Sasha's mind, the Hive resembled a ramshackle ribcage with some sort of puckering bone disease, covered in winking cloacas. A tumorous appendage to the shiny, loud, flat, featureless quality dominating the Midtown landscape's contemporary design. An aura of ultramodernity that would be laughably dated in approximately 15 minutes.

Sasha preferred a more classic aesthetic, the best she could achieve on her limited budget. She accessorized her studio apartment with discount-store damask curtains, library-sale leatherbound volumes, flea market daguerreotypes.

This aesthetic extended to her personal style: waistcoats and wingtips, pinstripes and pocket squares, short hair combed straight back with a hint of pomade, and a touch of lipstick or eye shadow on special occasions.

She aspired to look like a lightly feminized gentleman from a Leyendecker painting, but surrounded by the adoring gazes of sly, red-lipped sirens rather than fellow men. She liked to call her style 'bespoke butch' in the unlikely event she could someday afford a tailor.

At least the gilt-and-marble fixtures in the lobby of her century-old office building served as a brief Deco respite, one last holdout among the many industrial totems in rusting metal and cement, shards from a giant's shattered mirror, looming monolithic slabs.

After work one day on the edge of summer, Sasha nearly barreled into a trio of tourists who had crossed the street only to *stop*, stock-still, on the corner once menaced by Scabby the Rat. They were staring glazed-eyed at the bulbous form of the Hive, nestled within its skyscraper throne. One of them slowly raised his right arm and unfurled his index finger in the Hive's direction. None of them acknowledged Sasha or her muttered 'excuse me.'

This time she gave the Hive a more than contemptuous glance.

What, she wondered, was so goddamned fascinating?

The first thing that caught her eye was the distant pair standing in one of the Hive's topmost pods. Against the horizon they looked like insects—shadows of insects, really. Tiny malnourished larvae wavering limblessly in search of purpose.

She thought of her ex, Anita, the cocooned ghost moth. Anita's apartment was infested with the small, slim, drain-dwelling roaches euphemistically called 'water bugs.' Sasha would casually smash them with the flat of her hand as they scampered up the doorframe or out of the kitchen sink. She would wipe up the clusters of dun-colored poppy-seed shits they left in the cupboards. The water bugs—*roaches*—were likely still there, and more comfortably so, as far as Sasha knew.

Anita was curiously indifferent to certain aspects of routine life maintenance. Melted candles pooled on the floorboards, gathering months of dust; crumbs crushed into the creases of the futon; fruits and vegetables liquefying in the crisper. Her wavy hair, dyed a lush Tyrian purple, had faded weeks later into an ashy lavender with visibly dark roots she made no effort to touch up: not in an attempt at a fashionable ombre style, but out of pure laziness.

Yet Anita was successful enough in her job as a paralegal that she could afford to live alone in a modest one bedroom in a lightly gentrified neighborhood of an outer borough, and she took her SSRIs at 7 AM on the dot each morning. Perhaps Anita had absorbed the ethos of the graffiti-and-grime-encrusted Philly punk houses she had occupied during her early twenties, with their combined terroir of body odor, cigarette ash, and stale Pabst.

Lovely Anita, lounging on her crumb-laden futon in gauzy, curve-clinging dresses. Perhaps *laziness* was unfair. Perhaps it was more of a neurasthenic ennui: the polar opposite of the Hive's kinetic brand of tourism. She would've had some arch remark about that Guilford Gardens eyesore, no doubt.

It shouldn't have gone on quite so long as it did, Sasha knew, but good *god*, had they hated so many of the same things. That anxious twinge rising in her brain once again. *Move along, now, Lefkovich.*

Moving along, past the girders and scaffolding like an enormous child's Erector set. Did children still play with such things, physical toys? *Oh, come on,* she thought, *of course they do. You're not that out of touch.* She pictured herself as a fusty grandmother stroking a shotgun in front of a Unabomber shack. If only technology wasn't so ugly—and worse, ugly by design.

Well, if she had to see it every day, she considered, just once, taking a walk around the Hive's perimeter before going home. Make an informed decision about just how contemptuous she should be.

She wended her way past street-meat carts and vendors hawking bootleg Hive merchandise—t-shirts, buttons, framed prints, magnets—pushed to the edge of the public square in an uneasy truce between high and low commerce. Generic pop-rock blasted from someone's portable stereo, the singer boasting of his alleged *moo-oo-oo-oo-oo-oo-oo-oo-ooves* like Jagger.

Mick Jagger is a great-grandfather now, thought Sasha.

A spread of round metal tables across the concrete square went largely ignored by Hive gawkers, save one notable exception: an ash-blonde twenty something with the chap-cheeked, chinless toddler-face of Anna Delvey and the fussy, rectangular brows of a Kardashian, occupying a metal picnic chair with legs crossed in mesh-paneled yoga pants. She took polite sips of flavored seltzer with a cartoon dream catcher on the label, frowning into her phone and reapplying shiny gloss each time her thin lips left the bottle.

A slightly older man—boyfriend? handler? bodyguard?—with a beefy ex-jock physique stood in front of her, holding up a redundant ring light just behind her open laptop. She was clearly positioned such that the Hive would appear in her background.

"Heeee-ey! What's up, my lovelies?" she said into her webcam, pronouncing it more like luv-lays. "It's your BFF Mary-Lee Jasper here at the Hive in beautiful Midtown Manhattan and I. Am. *Shook!*"

Sasha chose to assume this girl's name was spelled as obnoxiously as possible: *Merralee Jaspurr? Maerrileigh Jazzpyr?* She continued to passively eavesdrop while observing her surroundings.

Guilford Gardens contained no actual gardens, no plant life of any kind beyond a few small, embarrassed trees and the incongruous floral-print tarps covering chain-link construction fences. The closest thing to a true garden was a long bed of grey gravel which, according to various small sans-serif placards, one was to refrain from stepping on or allowing one's dog to soil.

"Sooo, my besties at Jeunesse Spirit Water hooked me up with some swag," said Meer Alie, shaking the half-empty bottle, its label out front. "Um. *Shit.* Forgot to mention '*#HiveChallenge.*' Hold on, Mike, I'm gonna redo this take."

At Sasha's back loomed "The Moze."

Mosey on home, there, pard'ner, she thought in Anita's sardonic drawl.

Its glass doors were bracketed by huge ads in which poreless young giants with salon blowouts lolled about in artful dishevel, sexily bored. Sasha had read about this place, that they were employing a new cashless paradigm wherein guests would pay for everything with their phones. A co-worker had recently complained within Sasha's earshot of accidentally being charged double there for her $25 gourmet grilled cheese take-out lunch.

"Whatevs, it's a Capricorn thang," said Mare-a-Lay, cocking her head and flashing a peace sign.

A pendant made from a rough chunk of rose quartz bounced against the bedazzled letters in loopy font across the front of her crop top. Sasha had to squint to make out the words: DADDY'S GIRL. For all Sasha knew, she lived next door in a Tammany Tower condo. For all Sasha knew, she belonged to the same itinerant trustafarian set as the Hive's absent architect. For all Sasha knew, she was just another tourist.

And the scene was *crawling* with tourists.

Tourists with cloudy eyes like fish on ice. Tourists with limp, stringy limbs. Tourists with overly wide Sardonicus grins. All lined up like the segments of a twitching millipede for their first round—or their fortieth—minded by a team of masked and frock-coated watchmen positioned silently at entrance and exit. All either stiffly still or in constant motion, nothing in between.

The Hive's hollow interior was lined with stairs and landings but had no proper seats, such that all one could do was climb or descend. One *must* keep moving, a hamster's stubby paws working the wheel.

If there's one thing locals love, Sasha thought, *it's taking stairs unnecessarily.*

More of an aesthete than an athlete, Sasha could find herself winded from convoluted transfers between subway platforms, thus her curiosity only extended so far. At any rate, tickets were also required to enter: as in The Moze, one had to sign up with one's phone, and hers was frankly a piece of shit with an increasingly gravid battery.

A yellow-eyed man emerged from the Hive's back gullet, raising both fists, gushing of having made the trip several times today.

"I'm pumped I'm pumped *I'm pumped!!!*" he shouted, grinning at her, at everyone, like the most insufferable breed of coke fiend.

"Excuse me, sir—uh, ma'am?" said the guy with the ring light. It took a couple of beats before Sasha realized he meant her.

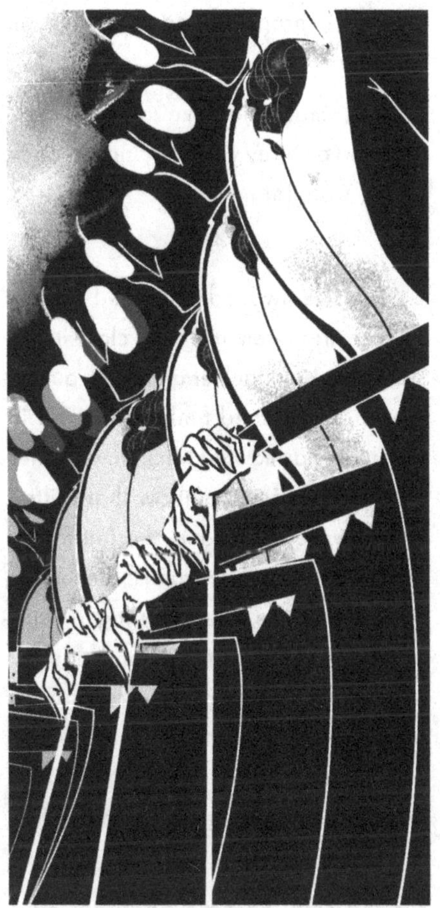

"Whatever."

"Excuse me, you're in her light. You're in Miss Jazzpyr's light."

Sasha blinked hard at the accusing glow of the harsh fluorescents, which did not bother the pouting blonde influencer, whose round-lensed sunglasses dominated half her face. And when Sasha didn't immediately react to the man:

"She has 59 *thou*-sand followers," he said, as if this explained anything.

Sasha shrugged and continued on her way.

"—so smash that 'like' and 'follow'!" resumed a chirpy voice behind her back. "TTFN: Ta-ta for now!"

The Hive awaited, anodized chrome in sickly iridescent hues. Up close it was somehow both tackier and more authoritarian, a polished funhouse mirror in which Sasha scowled back down at herself in an oil-slick rainbow that shifted of its own accord, and she felt faintly nauseated. Uncannily organic, the surface pulsed like the ever-splitting fractal-spire of hallucinogenic visions, rippling around the convex gaps, a ruin from a dream. A high-pitched electrical hum emitting from inside, a shift of warmth in the surrounding air, a charge. Hypnotic.

The humid air lifted, followed by a sudden chill. Sasha rubbed her eyes and felt as though time had glitched. The scene around her was unchanged, but the sky had visibly dimmed, with a sweaty discomfort in her various unseasonable layers, as though she'd been standing there far longer than the few seconds it had seemed. A Hive watchman had fixed his plague doctor's gaze onto Sasha, and she strode quickly back to the subway, a tinnitus-whine ringing faintly in her ear.

On the ride home, wedged in beside a slick-haired finance bro flipping intently through his various Hive selfies, she realized she couldn't picture these affluent tourists as having interior monologues, original thoughts, inner lives.

They were made to walk, to gawk, to make ephemeral documentation, to disappear forever. Had Sasha been plucked by the collar and deposited in Times Square or Ground Zero, the scene would differ only in set dressing, its background actors recycled interminably.

And she was a ghost among them— a slim, severe-figured, wasp-waisted, stern-faced, mildly eccentric, not fully masculine or feminine, not fully present or past.

In the office break room, Sasha drifted through the perpetual talk of sports and celebrities and superheroes to siphon mediocre-but-free coffee from a plastic carafe. Today, however, a sudden flash and blare interrupted this usual routine: the fire alarm.

Was this a planned fire drill she'd forgotten about? Many of her coworkers seemed to think so. As the bulk of them waited to cram themselves onto the elevator, Sasha darted into the stairwell, through the shabby guts of the building, out the service entrance.

Milling before the revolving doors as time slipped by, tension-relief joking began amongst her co-workers.

"Wonder if Teacher will let us have class outdoors today," said Steve from Accounts Receivable.

"Maybe we could do a power walk around the block, get some cardio in," said Jan from Reception.

As jokes and small talk began shifting into grumbles and worries, a man from the building's maintenance department stepped into the loose crowd, struggling to explain things in layman's terms. That there was "leakage in the underground pipes; um, some kinda groundswell interfering with the wiring." That this had sparked a small fire in the basement. That it was being taken care of.

Soon, a trio of grim laborers emerged from the service entrance with what looked like an unusually vivid gasoline spill spattered across their coveralls. A workman with a salt-and-pepper beard cast a baleful glance in the direction of Guilford Gardens.

Leaving the office a few hours later, Sasha passed a silver-haired tourist wiping something disagreeable off the bottom of his sensible sneakers, muttering in some Scandinavian language as his wife or girlfriend peered down with a troubled frown. Sasha noted with disapproval that apparently no one bothered to clean the Hive's plexiglass bubbles, which had grown cloudy with the detritus of rainwater and condensation and (quite likely) mildew, a reptile skin soon to loosen and shed.

A creature of routine, Sasha broke out of habit one weekend to attend her cousin's wedding on Long Island. The main factor that coaxed her, beyond free food and an open bar, was the wedding's setting in an opulent Gilded Age manor house on a sprawling parkland, rather than one of those garish neon-spangled milestone multiplexes where her older brother had held both his own wedding and his son's bar mitzvah.

At the reception, she sawed at a seasoned lamb chop, watching distant middle-aged relatives in love—or at least happy—longtime companionship with their average-looking spouses. It was a different world.

"No plus-one?" asked her brother's wife, eyebrow raised, a little smirk.

"Nope." Sasha didn't elaborate.

Later, tipsy, she fell into a lengthy conversation with her new cousin-in-law's bridesmaid from Salem, who was a professional reenactor at some historic site, a seasonal actress at a haunted house, and a freelance tarot reader.

The girl had reached over and straightened her ascot stickpin, fingertips lightly brushing her throat, with a wicked tint to her smile like Anita's, and Sasha felt her cheeks grow hot. Perhaps the re-enactor girl was flirting with her. Perhaps. How Sasha had rapped a knuckle against the hollow panel in one wall of the manor house, pointing out the discreet servants' entrance built under the stairs. How she could have, should have, suggested...

Back in her hotel room, drunk and alone, remembering how she had once danced with Anita, filmy fabric and warm sweat and the curve of her back, small nipples poking through, lipstick stains across Sasha's jawline, to the shimmering pulse of dark synth-pop at a DJ night in Bushwick at a bar that no longer existed and *why*, why think about it. In the end she was sort of a terrible person, wasn't she, they'd been too different but still, if only some great divine hand *ex machina* had reached down from the heavens to stop time, stay the inevitable for a while; and picturing this girl, the re-enactor whose name she couldn't even remember, in Anita's place, but this was too much hope, the moment was gone, dust in the wind.

You blew it, Lefkovich.

Honestly it was hard to meet girls in the city, especially girls who weren't already friends or acquaintances or ex-lovers of Anita's, tainted by association and its potential for drama. Those delicate, cringing responses on dating sites: that wasn't it a little, well, internally misogynistic/imperialist/cryptofascist/problematic to wear masculine-coded attire evoking vintage eras?

Golly, she thought, *should I pierce my nose like a bull and chop my hair into a sloppy bowl cut and wear nothing but lumpy bargain-bin cardigans in soothing pastels? Do you have to look like you were styled by a kindergartener with a pair of safety scissors to get a date these days?*

When will I be the protagonist in my own story and not an observer jotting down notes?

In the last mental haze before she fell asleep, an image of the reenactor knocking on lacquered wood in the hoop skirt, corkscrew curls, and black crape of an antebellum widow, a mad smile, an invitation: *Come, come! The servants' entrance!*

Autumn crept in, mist congealing into fog. The plodding rhythms of construction, a distant churn and rumble under the earth. A curdled murk of sky, the time of day impossible. Was she going to work or coming back?

Not sure. Not sure at all.

Beyond Sasha, the only pedestrians were there for the Hive. Uniformly grey and thin, waxen-skinned, clothing tattered, some fully naked. Nobody noticed or commented, merely stood and stared upward, surrounding the Hive in concentric circles. A constant sound emerged from inside, an amplified drone thrumming in layers.

The convex plexiglass panes were almost opaque now, straining against their frame like buboes at a plague victim's groin. The Hive dripped and burbled. A crooked arm moved weakly within a fallen clot of protoplasm, a token show of protest before going limp.

The ash-blonde influencer, now rasp-throated and mummy-thin, continued passing through the motions.

"Ehhh-ey. Ish Merrrlee," she said through bare gums, the laptop screen blackened and dead. A row of tiny teeth and manicured nails on the table before her, idly pushing them about into patterns. Her handler's head lolled back, jaw exposed on frayed hinges, legs dissolving into a burnt stain on the concrete beside the fallen blaze of the ring light.

As Sasha passed by, one of Mary-Lee's ears fell off and so did her sunglasses, revealing little worms that writhed in the empty pouches of her lower lids.

"'Ee 'ee eff em, 'ah-ah fuh 'ow."

The watchmen awaited in gloves and goggles, their coattails twitching, skinny arms drooped over matching black canes, flanking a wall of mottled meat.

'Come, come! The serpents' entrance!' A seductive woman's voice, carried on the wind.

And the cloaca rolled open. A gust of hot, fetid air, followed by a sharp chill in the opposite direction.

It was breathing.

The watchmen stood back, arms extended like circus impresarios, welcoming Sasha to the segmented intestinal curl of the Hive. She stepped forward, not yet inside. The membranes of its walls emitted a shifting inner glow, yet she could only see a few feet before her.

A heady supernal smog clotted the flesh tunnel with the half-faces of pedestrians in bowler hats and bonnets, flat caps and mob caps and baseball caps, top hats and cloches and the occasional tricorne, Edwardian ladies' hats like banquet platters, all absorbed from absent days, from the streets of the city itself, bones rotten to dark dirt layers upon layers under the concrete.

The mist receded just enough to let her see, several steps ahead, a visiting man gripped from both sides by the wet

muscles of the wall and forcibly thrust forward. Sasha, hurrying backwards, breaking the circle of grey bodies, understood the Hive's throbbing abdomen protruding from the earth implied a hidden thorax and head growing downwards, wheeling through the soil, devouring from beneath.

The convex pods now revealed as jellied eggs, glimpses of ghosts ebbing in and out, faces covered by cloth masks and mourning veils, niqabs and balaclavas, vinyl and plastic Halloween trappings.

And a stark, unforgettable glimpse of one beautiful feminine face with a sly smile, a gauze-draped frame, a twitch of wet wings.

She permitted one last glance back.

At the very top of the Hive stood the internet-famous form of Hamilton Chesebrough VI, come home to roost, if indeed he had ever left.

Twitching fingers unbuttoned his shirt, flaying the fabric in both hands to reveal a dripping honeycomb in his chest, soaking his ragged jeans with viscous nectar. He opened his mouth to shout, perhaps to preach, emitting only a painful static buzz.

Sasha stuffed her hands into her pockets and retreated into the subway, underground, back to a niche in a building of daubed dirt where the larvae curled up in the cracks and moorings, waiting.

STEPHANIE GRAY

THE SECRET OF THETA PI

We travel back to Tandy's Cove in a caravan of three, Cindy Q.'s Miata leading, followed by the rented van, dirty white with the windows rolled up, and Beneeta G.'s little blue hatchback bringing up the rear. Twelve hours on the road would be stressful in the best of times, yet in these days of turmoil there is an easy peace between us. Some of us, Linda B. who studies the languorous depths of the ocean and Karen G. who lives in libraries, cherish the silence, while others, sporty Beneeta G. and Mia L., begin to crave one of our petty squabbles just to break up this endless day.

Within the guarded confines of the van, Linda B. and Carolyn G. watch over our cargo while Suzy F. sleeps curled over the wheel well, lulled by the rhythm of the road. They lie low on the piled blankets that cover the scratchy floor, bodies parallel, hips pressed against the side of the 30-gallon Home Depot storage tub that houses our sloshing passenger, wrapped in bungee cords to keep it secured over rocky roads.

("All roads are rocky," says Carolyn G., who is a poet and in love.)

We drive on through the morning and afternoon without stopping. At four, burgers and fries at a truck stop McDonalds, stale coffee and cat-calls and taking turns in the restroom.

Mia L. without makeup, Cindy Q. with her phone turned off, homework backlogged, we are raw and real out here, alone with the tender truths of our sisterhood. We take turns guarding the van while we take in the oily truck stop air, bear the leers, lick the grease from our fingers, and move on, as quickly as we can.

We switch drivers, Carolyn G. taking control of the van so Karen G. can doze. We regain cell phone service about twenty miles from the ocean and text each other constantly, making up ever-changing call-signs (*"Duck-Face to Purple Haze, do you read me?"*) to lighten the mood.

Ever since spring break, Lorna had been acting differently. Cindy Q. swore it was the introspective aftermath of a spring fling and Beneeta G., the nervous excitement of graduation and the oncoming summer.

"Is it her grades?" Karen G. asked, "She's missed so many classes."

"There's more to life than grades, sweetie," said Cindy Q., pursing her lips in the hallway mirror as she got ready for a date.

"Is she still with Colt?" Carolyn G. asked, "She never said they broke up, but I haven't seen him around."

No one had a clear answer, and when posed with the question herself, Lorna always seemed to sidestep the topic, drifting away through the mysterious seascape she'd seemed to inhabit since returning from Tandy's Cove. She slept late, missing classes as often as she attended them. Divesting herself of her formerly cluttered social calendar, she retreated inward, spending days barricaded in her bedroom in Theta Pi house, nested in blankets despite the warm weather. She would leave only to venture cautiously to the kitchen to find food, or to shower, which she did religiously, often two or three times a day.

"Drugs?' Linda B. wondered cautiously, peering up from her Deep-Sea Ecology notes.

"No," said Mia L., six months past her own collapse in a downtown nightclub and the sticky, waiting-room morning that followed. "She'd have told me."

It was Carolyn G. who first ventured into Lorna's bedroom, breaking through the barricades to reach the secret heart of the matter. Carolyn G. who'd been crippled by secrets long before any of us knew her, and to whom we were all grateful.

"It's okay," she told Lorna, their fingers threading together in the dark. "It doesn't matter what it is, you can tell us. We're all here for you. We love you." It was the truth, despite the open secret that set Carolyn G.'s love apart.

But Lorna stayed silent as the tomb-like depths of the ocean, and we women of Theta Pi had no choice but to make a reluctant retreat.

But the tide always turns, and by the end of March, Lorna was almost back to her old self again. She returned to her classes, haggled with professors for make-up assignments, coloured in her social calendar with parties and dates.

"I told you she'd get over it," said Cindy Q. "Sometimes you just need your space."

But Carolyn G. remembered the wet press of Lorna's palm against her own, the tangy scent despite her constant showers. "Something's still not right."

It wasn't until Easter weekend that we learned how true those words really were.

Suzy F., the lightest sleeper, was the one who heard Lorna crying in the laundry room. Always crowded and cluttered during the day, a canopy of hanging bras, nylons draped over open doors, the room was nearly eerie in the cavernous silence of three a.m. Lorna was bowed over the laundry sink, scrubbing, hands submerged in dark, soapy water.

"What are you doing in here?" Suzy F. asked.

"It's fine," Lorna said, "It's nothing. Go back to bed"

Suzy F., who'd spent more late and messy nights than she could bear to count hiding dark secrets of her own, knew the frantic energy and desperation it took to believe it was possible to scrub away reality. Suzy F. did not go back to bed. Instead she walked up beside Lorna, laid a hand on her tense, clammy shoulder. Submerged in the water, Lorna's hands had turned blotchy purple, stained and traumatized by the harsh chemicals.

Lorna's tears felt oddly cold as they landed on Suzy F.'s bare shoulder.

Many cephalopods, Linda B. would tell us later, squirt ink when excited or afraid, to blind and confuse their enemies. However, similar to the weapons of the warm blooded, the ink is more than capable of poisoning those whom it was meant to defend.

"I could have told you that," said Suzy F.

In the evening, just outside the camp grounds, we pass a road check, and it is the most terrifying moment of our lives. Fumbling for seatbelts, a cacophony of whispers urging each other to be silent. We throw a blanket hastily over the plastic storage bin, purses piled on top of it to obscure its presence. The sloshing inside suddenly sounds like the churning of rapids.

Carolyn G. smiles out the window at the flashlight shining into her face.

"Where are you ladies headed? Anything to drink tonight?"

She answers back in a low, steady voice, "We're just going camping, officer. No, nothing to drink, officer."

We breathe a sigh of relief as the flashlight withdraws and we hear those precious words, like a balm to our panic: "That's fine, ladies. Drive safe tonight."

Thus freed, the engine churns to life and we head on towards the ocean.

Beneeta G. led the charge, storming down fraternity row with strength of purpose burning in her all-loving, warrior's heart. She knocked on the door for nearly five minutes, using the toe of her hiking boot when her knuckles got sore, until finally it opened on a bleary, hungover undergrad.

"Is Kevin here?" Beneeta G. asked, all toned and tattooed six feet of her with her arms crossed and a steel-spined golf umbrella clutched in her manicured hand.

The undergrad stepped away, pointing them up to Kevin's room through the beery detritus of a party, most of the Sigma Omega boys still sleeping if they hadn't stumbled off to class.

We burst into Kevin's room to the stench of beer and gym socks and Kevin, sitting in bed in his boxer shorts and ICP t-shirt, bandaged hand fumbling with the tab on a breakfast beer. A startled jolt, spraying foam, then anger.

"What the fuck are you bitches doing here? Get the fuck out of my room."

"What happened with Lorna?" Beneeta G. demanded.

"Did she send you here?" asked Kevin, "What did that bitch tell you? She's fucking lying."

We didn't budge, and we didn't back down. We'd been there for each other through bad grades and break-ups and other, darker horrors. We'd fought each other's battles in hospital waiting rooms and funeral parlours, on the darkest frontiers of our most secret lives. We'd stood by Suzy F., when it happened to her, and we'd stand by Lorna now.

"It's all fucking Colt's fault. He's the one who left her there. I only went after her because he said she was a fucking freak, I didn't think he meant ..." His face turned a shade of green.

"Where is Colt?" Beneeta G. asked, "I thought he dropped out."

"He did." Kevin shouted, "Thanks to *her*. Who wouldn't have, after what happened in Tandy's Cove?"

"What *did* happen in Tandy's Cove?" said Mia L., glaring, hands on her hips.

"You don't know?" His eyes widened, some glimmer in them like genuine sympathy, something else crushing it down. "I only know what Colt told me, alright?"

"What did Colt tell you?" asked Cindy Q., idly brushing a layer of dust off the top of the DVD wrack as she examined the titles in disgust. Kevin looked down at his damaged hand.

"They'd gone out skinny dipping, late at night. Colt was just fooling around, but Lorna started freaking out and running away from him. She slipped, fell into the water over where it was deep. He thought she'd come up, but ... he said it looked like something grabbed her, pulled her down."

He took a deep breath, staring blankly at the cracked plaster next to his bed, a roofing nail holding up a Playboy centerfold.

"He swore he thought she was dead."

"He abandoned her?" asked Mia L., who'd once flagged down her own cab to the hospital when her date refused to leave the party.

"He knew how it would have looked," Kevin said, "The guy always gets blamed."

Cindy Q. rolled her eyes.

"He went back for her, as soon as he got cell service back and got her messages, he went back and got her."

"What a fucking hero," said Mia L. as she and Beneeta G. shared an incredulous glance.

"It's what happened on the way back that I didn't believe," Kevin said, seizing another beer from the mini fridge next to the bed, "I thought it must have been Lorna fucking with him, you know, for revenge or something." He points with his bandaged finger, "Your friend is one fucked up chick, you know that?"

"What happened?" asked Beneeta G.

"It was in the motel room, on the way back. Colt said she was all over him, nothing beats 'I almost died' sex, am I right?"

We refrain from commenting, forcing Kevin to move on.

"He was pushing her legs back, you know, and one of them went *all* the way back."

"What?" said Cindy Q.

THE SECRET OF THETA PI

"Not 'all the way back' as in 'been doing a lot of yoga'," Kevin replied, "I mean, as in 'My legs have no fucking bones in them.' He thought he'd broken her leg except ... there was no snap, no resistance. It just flopped back like it was made of fucking rubber. She was a fucking mutant."

"And you believed all that?" Cindy Q. wanted to know.

"No," Kevin said, still not looking at any of us, "Not at first. Then last night ..."

"What happened?" Beneeta G. asked, "What did you do?"

"You want to know what I did?" Kevin shouted. "What I *fucking did*?" He held up his bandaged hand. "I lost a fucking finger is what I did. Why don't you ask Lorna?"

Back at Theta Pi house, Suzy F. was sitting on the floor with her back pressed against the bathroom door, Lorna locked inside.

"Whatever happened," we told her, "we'll deal with it together."

When we finally unlocked the door, we found Lorna sitting on the edge of the bathtub, her skin the same colour as the porcelain. Unable to help ourselves, we glanced at her bare feet on the tile floor, observing the clear and precise outline of her bones. "I think there's something wrong with me."

Carolyn G. knelt down by the edge of the bath, placed a hand gently on Lorna's bare knee. Her skin felt slick and rubbery, cold to the touch. Lorna, trembling, pulled the hem of her skirt up to her hips and parted her legs.

From between the wet, pink folds of flesh slowly emerged something ridged and black, hooked and sharp as a knife.

"What is it?" asked Karen G., ever the scholar.

"I think it's a beak," said Linda B.

Lorna dissolved into tears.

The changes came more quickly after that. Lorna craved water constantly; when the water from our taps began to make her sick, Linda B. brought home a hydrometer and jugs of marine salt mix from the biology lab on campus and filled up the bathtub. At first Lorna only slept in it, but soon she couldn't bear to leave it at all. She kept us company while we brushed our teeth, sat on the toilet, took turns washing our hair in the sink.

We never minded sharing the space: we told her jokes, whispered secrets, rambled on about school or bad dates or post-graduation plans, just as we always had. Each day, each of us would lean over the edge of the bath and let her place her hands against the skin of our arms. Gradually, her bones dissolved into the rubbery flesh of her limbs, surprising everyone but Linda B. by how strong they were when they rose out of the water to embrace us. Tiny suckers grew on the pads of her hands that left tiny red hickies on our skin wherever she'd touched us.

Her skin became poreless and pliant, then translucent as smoked glass. That part was the hardest, because of what it allowed us to see: the distorted outline of her spine as it shrank and shortened, vertebra by vertebra, until it was gone.

She showed us pictures on her skin, galaxies of colour and patterns, red and orange sunbursts when she was happy and deep indigo when she was feeling melancholy. And when we were sad, for her or for ourselves, she would reach out of the tub and coil one of her lengthening limbs around our arms, or lay a suckered finger against our cheeks, leaving her tiny red kisses, heart-shaped, upon our skin. In these ways we were able to communicate with her, in a fashion, long after her mouth had sealed itself shut, grown over by a thickening membrane of rubbery flesh.

What would only seem miraculous in hindsight was what small aspects of her human form remained for long after they seemed like they should have gone. Her hair, perpetually wet but combed and braided daily by Cindy Q., didn't fall out until after she had become almost entirely boneless. When it finally began to come out strand by strand in Cindy Q.'s comb, we were all careful not to cry in front of Lorna, baffled by how this, of all things, could seem so final.

She ate rarely, which Linda B. assured us was to be expected, and only when alone. She would take the fresh crayfish Linda B. brought home for her, pass them along her suckers, hand to hand, but she wouldn't take them beneath the water towards her beak until we were all gone. We looked to Linda B. for an explanation, some factoid of Pacific cephalopod behaviour that would justify this.

"I think she's embarrassed," Linda B. said, and we all burned with shame.

When summer came, after much discussion and even more divining of Lorna's new kaleidoscopic skin, we moved her from the bathtub and into a forty gallon plastic trash can full of salt water. From there, we transported her to the campus marine biology lab to which Linda B., recently accepted by a summer internship program, now had 24-hour access.

We used to sit with her, just watching her colours change as she drifted lazily amongst the coral and imported algae, the bright, flashing silver of the fish with whom she shared her tank. Sometimes we played music for her, and she would pattern her skin in rhythm to demonstrate her delight. We would open her tank often, and she would emerge to embrace us, leaving her wet, slick kisses on our skin. Sometimes she splashed water at us, turned a friendly orange, playful. At other times she surfaced slowly, or not at all, her colour a muddy green.

"What if she's unhappy here?" Carolyn G. asked, on a day when Lorna's skin was as smoky grey as the artificial rocks that lined the bottom of her tank, "The tank is so small. How long can we keep her in there?"

As the days grew longer, graduation approaching, and Lorna surfaced to embrace us with ever diminishing frequency, it was a question that had never been far from our minds.

"Her hands haven't changed yet," Linda B. observed. This was true, something we had all noticed. Her front two tentacles still forked into five at their very ends, maintaining the loose and boneless shape of human hands. As Lorna settled into her new form, we wondered if they would ever change.

At midnight, we carry her to the water. We take turns in pairs hefting the heavy,

sloshing container, as careful with it as we would be with a newborn babe. We drag it up onto the rocks, our hiking boots unsteady on the smooth, wet ground. We all look around for the best place to stop, until finally our flashlights converge on a wide crevice between two rocks, filled in by the lapping tide.

We lower Lorna's container into the crevice until its lip is level with the water. We unsnap the lid, and Lorna extends an exploratory tentacle, flashing a happy crimson as she tastes the sea.

One at a time, we kneel down before the parcel of ocean Lorna inhabits, letting her embrace us each one final time. Her kisses upon our cheeks we will cherish forever, even as they fade.

"Lorna," Carolyn G. whispers as Lorna's suckers pop softly against her face, tasting her warm salt tears, "We'll never forget you."

Lorna extends her six tapered tentacles into the ocean and slowly pushes herself over the lip of the container, out into the vastness of the open sea. Her two tentacles that still fork into five fingers, unique among all the creatures of the ocean, are the last to slide over the edge of the tub. They rise up out of the water just once before she departs, giving us a final wave.

We wait there on the rocks for a long time, staring out into the ocean, wondering if we will ever see her again.

DIANA FENVES

THE LONG SLEEP

— OCTOBER —

Hugo's mom said goodbye to him in the Waffle House parking lot with a long, hard hug and a wet kiss on his cheek. She'd been crying, which always made Hugo ache inside. He smiled his widest, most adorable smile to comfort her, but it only made her sob harder. Her eyes teared up so much her nose ran, and she rubbed it with the back of her hand with a lack of dignity that was unusual for her.

"I've got to go, baby."

"It's okay, Mom."

He squared his shoulders like he'd seen his older cousin do, to show that he could be strong and sturdy even if he was only 9. Still, 9 wasn't so little. His mom let him cook dinner sometimes now, like just-add-water mac n' cheese, and salads with the food they got from the community garden down the street by the small icky pond he called "Mosquito Lake." He wasn't allowed to chop veggies without her supervision, but he could use the airgrill and the flip-pot to make soups and hot drinks.

Winter was Hugo's favorite time, when the Durham sky finally lost its humid flush and the scary trees bordering their neighborhood got thin and near see-through. They usually spent the season drinking hot chocolate out of worn old mugs, their handles worn and familiar. Hugo got to sleep late; his mom relaxed in the dark hours of the morning.

This winter, he knew, would be different. Mom got another job, which meant more money, which was a good thing. But he couldn't come with her. He didn't like the idea, his mom being somewhere he couldn't picture. He liked being able to hold an image in his mind. His mom showed him pictures of the Center where she'd be—not far, just a few hours into the mountains, out near Asheville. She splurged, using up a lot of their data on a 3D projection of where she'd be working. She showed him the bright walls of the Center and the faces of all the smiling kids.

She'd be in training through the end of the fall, then come winter, she'd take care of children while their parents took the long sleep through the cold months and woke up like fairy tale creatures at the end of the season, skin smooth and radiant for spring. Hugo hated those children with their shining faces and nice clothes. Just because they couldn't be with their mothers, did they have to take his?

He asked at first if he could blend in among them. His mom shook her head sadly. He didn't ask why because he knew. The children in the photos were mostly pale and freckled, not like Hugo's caramel complexion, a few shades darker than his mom's pale olive.

"What if I'm real quiet?"

He'd gotten in trouble the last year in school for being a know-it-all and yelling answers at the prompter out of turn. Once, he tipped his desk over, hating how he was too grown-up for the little ramshackle table and chair. It dug into the tops of his thighs and cut into his back, keeping him rooted where he didn't want to be while the teacher's voice came out from the screens and speakers, always too slow and boring for Hugo's taste. But he could change. If he could go to the mountains, he would.

His mom had explained a dozen times why he couldn't go, until eventually Hugo stopped asking, because he noticed how her body sagged when she answered him, like it was collapsing in on itself.

They'd planned to send him to his Aunt Sarah's in Raleigh, but she'd gotten a step up, too. Her bosses' superiors were taking the long sleep, so just like that, everyone would be moving on up the line. She couldn't look after him, since she'd be moving to a nice corporate apartment that didn't allow pets or dependents for employees with less than five years seniority. Hugo was secretly relieved.

THE LONG SLEEP

Aunt Sarah made him watch cartoons on an old 2D display, insisting that more advanced technology would rot his brain. She seemed determined to get him interested in old moldy paperbacks with peeled faces and sad black-and-white insides. Plus, she snored real loud, and he didn't like her girlfriend who kept plying him with sticky candies that got stuck in his teeth.

Instead, his mother wrapped him up in more layers than were strictly necessary, including a humiliating hat with a large poofy ball on top, and drove him to his father's.

Hugo kept a picture of his dad in his head. A tall skinny man named Muhammad who lived in West Durham, where Hugo had once seen fancy cows on a school field trip. As a result, Hugo's inner-picture always showed his father surrounded by the fat, fuzzy, brown-and-white tufted animals. Sometimes he liked to add a cowboy hat and place his father on the back of one of the big beasts, his hands around a saddle horn. Hugo had been a fan of cowboys until he learned about astronauts, which were infinitely better, even if they didn't have animals.

Hugo sweated the whole drive over, as it couldn't have been colder than 60 degrees Fahrenheit this October afternoon. He stared at his mom's swollen suitcases with their forest green floral embroidery and worn seams. He cried the whole way, but not too loudly, just in case being quiet really was the key to sticking by his mom's side.

Hugo cried often, so it wasn't unusual for him to be sniffling. Not for any reason in particular, except that he felt like he had to. He didn't even notice it. He'd be playing outside, running up in circles around the apartment complex, training for his own future mission to Venus or Saturn, when he'd feel the wet tears spattering his wrists. He'd run harder until his sadness faded into a background noise at the back of his skull, and his toes bled in his too-small shoes.

The drive took more than an hour, since Mom had to keep pulling over and smacking the solar plate at the top of their Honda Civic to keep it working. Power surging through the car in fits and starts made the dashboard light up in glimmering colors. Hugo likened it to the bright consoles of spaceships on PBS specials, when the displays lit up and undulated like a living intelligence, guiding hibernating astronauts through the vacuum black of space and deftly swerving around rocky moons and metallic asteroids.

The Civic came to a rumbling stop outside a Waffle House off of 147. Muhammad—"Dad," or even "Father" seemed a little too familiar a name for such a brooding figure—leaned against the grimy windows, hands stuck into his armpits like he was cold.

Hugo, on the other hand, had sweat through his jacket and scarf. The tears left salty marks on his chin. He was too wet and gummy to see a man as significant as his father, a man so immensely important his appearance was strictly reserved for holidays, birthdays, and rare surprise visits where he rewarded Hugo with gifts and lifted him up, so he could be as regal and imposing as Muhammad.

His mother left him in the back seat for a whispered conference complete with heated gestures. His mom's face wrinkled into an all-over frown and Muhammad stared at the car, eyebrows up like he'd been expecting someone other than Hugo in the back seat.

"I've got a job, okay! I told you!"

Embarrassed by his own shout, his father immediately turned his back to Hugo and bent to whisper something in his mom's ear, which must have worked, because her frown eased, and she leaned into his arms for a while. It impressed Hugo enough to halt his crying, and he instead focused on re-picturing his parents. This time they sat beside him, and all three were drinking hot chocolate through the dry winter months.

His mother brought Hugo out of the car, picking him up despite his nine years and handling him like an infant, which Hugo didn't protest at all. He allowed himself to be gingerly transferred and set down by the restaurant door. She grabbed Hugo's Batman duffle bag from the Honda's trunk, upsetting the solar panel again. Muhammad spent a while fixing it while his mother went through the duffle, confirming Hugo had everything he needed. Then she threw her arms around Hugo in a long embrace, before heading up towards the mountains.

Hugo and his father watched the car get back on the highway in complete silence. Hugo's hands were gloved in puffy blue mittens, and Muhammad's were adorned with silver bands.

At last, Muhammad put his hand on Hugo's shoulder, making him hunch forward awkwardly, and quietly asked, "You hungry?"

Muhammad stretched out his friend's window, a wifi wand in his hand, trying to redirect the neighbor's internet. Hugo could see the muscles in his forearm twitching below the skin.

"Got it!"

Muhammad's friend Tomas shouted, and the picture finally cleared on their projection set. The astronauts' faces

THE LONG SLEEP

were coming into focus. Hugo leapt to his feet when Jamie Marcus' face came into view. He reached his hands through the projection to touch Jamie's white NASA uniform. He got up close to the set to look into Jamie's eyes.

"Sit down kid!"

"Let him."

Muhammad's commanding tone sounded from the window, firm but not loud. They'd been staying at Tomas' for the last week.

Muhammad's place wouldn't let him in, the welcome screen on the front door announcing a change in rent and dispensing a single one-night housing voucher paired with an eviction notice. Muhammad banged on the complex doors with his fists demanding an explanation, until the whole building went into lockdown and announced the authorities had been contacted.

He left Hugo at Tomas' while he worked, his hours constantly fluctuating and confusing Hugo's internal clock. Muhammad barely slept, instead spending his minuscule off-time either wolfing down instasmoothies right from the foil packet or praying on the worn carpet he always had with him.

Hugo filled most afternoons tuned into lessons on his tablet, both relieved that his mom had gotten him out of the classroom for the rest of the year, but also strangely missing the familiar halls of school, not to mention the warm breakfast they got twice a week.

Tomas' place didn't have much food in it, and Tomas' mother wouldn't let Hugo cook on his own, not trusting him to leave the living room. He practiced long strides, working on his wide-paced low-gravity walk and jumping up and down to build muscle strength. He spent hours with Tomas' cats, trying to learn their language of hisses.

The only relief was knowing that soon, they'd send the next broadcast from the Mars mission. The final broadcast before the crew went down for another eighteen months of sleep, at least. Hugo, ignoring the tablet's instructions, spent most of his days listening to Jamie Marcus' video channel.

Jamie wore bright Byzantine blue, glittering eyeshadow and thick silver lipstick. Jamie spoke with a deep, confident voice. Sometimes the videos were about science and all the wonders of space. Sometimes it felt like a diary full of personal details about what Jamie's hopes for Mars were, and how they'd worked their whole life to get there. With skin light-brown and an athletic frame, the astronaut glowed with confidence and charm.

A legend made real.

In all of Hugo's pictures of his future self, he looked just like that and ran, comfortably, even in space boots, across the wide Mars desert. He would race Jamie to one of NASA's white domes, his limbs long and proud like his father's, and all his movements dignified, like his mom's.

In Hugo's picture of Mars, NASA's dome rose like a castle from the red-clay soil, and all the astronauts stared at him wistfully from inside their helmets, wishing they were as fast and as smart as he was. Hugo learned the final video would be projected to Earth as quickly as satellites could bounce the signal—

a time lag of only a few hours. This was the closest Hugo had ever come to hearing Jamie's real-live voice.

Jamie's face filled the screen. They winked at the camera, showing off eyeshadow that shimmered between a brilliant gold and a mysterious fuchsia.

Jamie pouted, "Oh, it's hard being so far from home. We can see the Earth from here and to us the whole planet is the size of a dime. Imagine! We're conducting our final tests here. You can see my bonsai experiment is going well. My tree, Yoshi, is growing nicely using my new formula of Mars minerals. I can't wait to try it out in the dome.

"All that's left is to put the finishing touches on my hibernation mix. Thank you, all you blessed Earthlings at home, who have sent me recommendations. I've settled on a mix of language learning, my favorite equations and some electroreggae from home, and yes, Mom, I'm including your very own jazz selections and early 2000's alt-rock.

"I'm also including guest lectures for my crewmates on all their specialties and free lectures courtesy of Yale University to broaden my horizons. Y'all can download my list from NASA.org with promocode MARS #35. It's free for the next 24 hours thanks to our sponsor, Amazon.

"Before I hand it over to Sasha, I want to send all you on planet Earth my everlasting love. Wish me sweet dreams, America!"

They kissed their manicured hand and blew a glistening lipstick kiss to the screen.

The feed switched to the ship's exterior, showing off the luminous control panels before going suddenly dark.

"Shit!" Tomas yelled.

"No cursing!" his mother said, reaching over too late to cover Hugo's ears.

Muhammad folded himself back inside the living room.

"I can't get it back."

"Our data's maxed out. Neighbors too, probably. And just in time for *tus primos* to visit. They'll complain."

"Who are *primos*?" Hugo asked, hungry for information as always.

— NOVEMBER —

A week later they were sleeping in Muhammad's SUV. His father put the back seat down and covered it in blankets to make it more comfortable. He even plugged the car into the outlet of a mall parking lot so they could have power all night. He kept the heat on low and played soothing ocean sounds through the stereo.

"It's like we're on a boat," said Hugo.

"That's right. This is our ship."

"Can we be pirates?"

"Pirates steal. Let's be sailors, instead."

"Okay, but only if I get to be Captain."

"Yes, Captain."

"Yes, Captain, *sir*."

"Yes, Captain, sir."

Hugo giggled. His tall father called him sir.

They'd left Tomas' place that afternoon before the relatives arrived to take their place on the plaid couch. Tomas' mother had hugged him before he left and given him a box of Sour Patch Kids. He ate so many, his tongue went numb and sugar-burnt. She'd also given him a box of mouth-watering arepas con queso, which he ate so quickly he'd almost thrown up. Muhammad, who he'd started calling "Dad," had tried to make him slow down, but he couldn't keep himself from greedily lapping up the cheese sandwich.

Hugo jumped around the SUV searching for pirates, until his father shouted at him to sleep. He curled up under the covers, while his dad reclined in the front seat. He shut his eyes tight and tried to call up one of the pictures of his mom. The one he created for himself where she made gingerbread houses with the smile-faced children at her new job.

When he still couldn't sleep, his fists tightening with jealousy, he thought instead about Jamie asleep in the space shuttle. Twinkling eyelids shut and strong arms crossed over his chest like a dozing pharaoh sailing through the pitch black of space.

A bright light and bang woke him up. He jumped awake, looking for pirates, or his mother, or a gunshot, or an asteroid. A police officer knocked on the car door with the butt of his flashlight. Muhammad woke up, quickly throwing his hands in front of his face, but the knocking didn't stop. The officer opened the door of the car with the override code and dragged his father out.

Hugo dived under the covers, eyes still blurry with sleep. He lay still, counting his heartbeats, hands clasped tightly around his elbows, nails digging into his skin.

His father came back a while later.

"I'm sorry, we can't stay here. Put on your seatbelt."

"Why can't I go back to my mom?"

"You can't yet."

"Why not? Because my mom's working?"

"Your mom's okay. But she's been in a car accident."

"Can I see her?"

THE LONG SLEEP

"You've got to stay here while your mom gets better. It'll be okay, alright? I'll take care of everything."

Hugo conjured the car up in his mind. Too many pictures started to form. The car flying off a mountain and into great, towering pine trees. His mother suspended in the air, cold rushing into the car through shattered windows and white snowflakes sticking to her long, dark hair.

— DECEMBER —

Muhammad took Hugo to the Smoothie King, where he worked extra shifts on top of his concessions job at the Bull City stadium. He gave Hugo an enormous, smelly kale shake to drink.

Once he'd checked that Hugo had finished the revolting, green vitashake, he led Hugo into the back room. He picked up a plastic bag. Fearing another lemongrass snack, Hugo stared glumly at the Target bag.

"Cover your eyes."

"I don't want to."

"Please."

Hugo covered his eyes in that sneaky way that ensured he could still see in between his lashes and through the gaps of his fingers. His father pulled out the helmet first—metal, sleek and magnificent in the fluorescent light.

"A helmet!"

An entire suit emerged from inside the bag. With Jamie's name written on the back. "Is that for me?"

"Yes, it's for you."

His father bent down so his face could be level with his son's.

"I want you to know that every day, every single day you're with me."

"I know."

Hugo smiled, too busy trying on the suit to say anything, happy to hear his father speak only to him and not to anyone else. He played quietly 'til the end of his father's shift. He drew invisible lines from all the corners of the room and its furniture. A thin line from the shiny corner of the AC unit, another from the edge of a brown sofa, plus a curved arc following the edge of the light overhead. He jumped carefully in the spaces between the perilous lines, twisting his arms and legs, almost dancing in his suit across the surface of a dangerous planet.

The next morning, Hugo had to drink yet another terrible smoothie in the backseat of the car. He'd spent the previous night curled up in the passenger's seat while mosquitoes flew through the open windows and devoured him.

He didn't hear his father say anything, but he caught sight of him in the rearview mirror. His eyes were puffy and tearing up as they slowly made their way onto I-147. Cars honked at them and angrily passed them in the left lane as they ambled along. They stopped at an unremarkable building behind Durham Tech.

The Durham "Sweet Dreams" Hibernation Center used to be a tobacco processing factory once, like so many buildings in town. With its rusty-colored brick, creamy mortar, and boxy sides, it could be the Community Center or even Hugo's School Testing Center.

Outside on the cracked sidewalk, an older woman sang in Spanish in front of a handful of lit candles. Her white hair was swept back in an embroidered handkerchief with faded red flowers. A couple sat beside her with a sign, "Work for Cash. Need Help with Wake Up."

Another woman, not so old, jumped in front of them on their way to the door.

"Can you spare any change? I have to get my baby. I only need fifty more for the wake-up fee."

Hugo stepped back, but Muhammad moved him forward, past the woman. A bearded man in a tie-dye shirt with beaded, blonde dreads handed them pamphlets as they walked toward the door.

"Thank you for helping Mother Earth, man!"

Muhammad walked coolly by him, but Hugo tugged one of his dreads, not able to keep from the temptation of stealing a sparkly bead. But the beads were secure in the man's hair, and he glared at Hugo with pink, dilated eyes.

Muhammad yanked him through the front door and inside, past a large display of a gorgeously sad woman in a negligee that read "Depressed? Skip Winter."

"These are the weekly maintenance rates for a child of his size, with the hibernation initiation fee broken up over the first few months. There's the cycle payments. Then there's the standard wake-up, clean-up, and revitalize fees. None of that includes any extension payments or maintenance costs since he'll only be with us for the season."

Inside the free-consultation booth, Muhammad went over the numbers again with the Intake Specialist. She was a round woman with verdant cat-eye glasses and bleached hair that framed her face. She took notes on a fancy, credit card thin tablet and tapped the screen with her manicured fingers. Her formal suit jacket almost concealed the sleeve of tattoos that crept up her arm.

THE LONG SLEEP

"I don't remember the wake-up package being so much."

"You're a former guest?" The intake specialist looked up.

"A while back. I was in the second-chance program."

"We lost funding for inmates. But this is still a heavily subsidized rate and as you see, there's an economical payment plan."

"It's just for the season. To be clear."

The intake specialist nodded and turned to Hugo. Her pink lipstick was somewhat disappointing when compared to Jamie's bold, metallic choices. Hugo vowed that when he was older he would never wear such a boring color. He considered pastels beneath him.

"What recordings would you like, young man? Do you want to see our selection?" She gestured to a shelf by her desk. "We've got our 510c3s, those are free, like 'The Road to Self-Sufficiency,' 'Dealing with Debt,' 'Jesus Saves,' and 'The Biography of Martin Luther King Jr.' Then there are some mostly musical ones, I think there's a Disney one left—"

"I want what the astronauts have. I'm going to be an astronaut."

"You know it hardly matters. I mean like only a teeny-tiny percentage of people even remember what they hear, much less process—"

"You heard him. What NASA gives them."

"Sir, what I'm saying is, we don't have that."

"I downloaded Jamie's playlist. I have it!" Hugo piped up, suddenly focused. He'd used his father's monthly data allowance getting it onto his tablet. Muhammad hadn't even yelled, just shook his head like he was too tired to be angry.

"You can use the recording, can't you?"

Muhammad kept pressing until the woman agreed. He signed all the paperwork, using a pen on real-life printed paper. Hugo had to put his thumbprint on one, marveling at how the ink felt sticky on his skin.

Hugo kept picking at the chair arms, but his father brought his chin up so he could look him in the eyes.

"I've done this before. It'll be alright. It's just for a few months until I can save enough to get us a place. Then your mom will be better. And we'll wake you up together. You won't even remember this time."

His father hugged him until the lady motioned him to leave. He wouldn't go—instead, he stood there until the plump blonde woman took Hugo's hand and led him to the prep room.

He turned behind him and craned his neck to see Muhammad staring at him, looking worried and surprisingly small in the intake office's large pleather chair. Hugo hugged his plastic Target bag to his chest, making certain his spacesuit was secure.

They stopped in a conference room with a row of low benches, like a church without an altar. Other people were already sitting there. A weeping woman sat with her shoulders hunched over like two round lumps beside her hanging head. A whole family sat holding hands and praying in Spanish. They wore faded jean shorts and T-shirts with "Henson's Farm" written on them. A couple wearing long tunics and woven sandals leaned together, hands linked and faces shut in a closed, pinched look.

Hugo saw another girl his age with red, frizzy hair flowing from her shoulders, her face alight with lovely pink freckles. Hugo sat behind her and stared at her halo of fiery hair, until she spun around to stare back at him.

Hugo put on pajamas as instructed, annoyed with the rough feeling of the fabric and its ugly puke-green checker print. The signs on the walls proclaimed that he was about to undertake a miraculous journey, but the models in the photos were wearing silken nighties and looked a lot happier than anyone Hugo had seen so far.

He'd already taken some pink, chalky tablets. The foul sweet kind that pretended to taste like cherry but didn't. He put his spacesuit on top of his pj's but held his helmet tucked under his arm like Jamie walking to the launchpad.

They led the little redheaded girl out first. Her hair was messed up from the clothing change and sticking out like a bird's nest. He ducked past the nurses to follow her. No one stopped him as he padded carefully behind her, his cotton booties gliding across the tile floor.

The hallway poured out into a vast warehouse even bigger than the gym his mom went to on Saturday mornings.

Rows and rows of pods filled the floor, their crystals clouded and cracked. Above them, a makeshift second level had been built out of steel pipes and laminate. Cords hung from this second level, wrapping around the pods and zigzagging across the floor in twisted lines and lumps.

Most pods had small monitors attached to them with dull grey-green screens like the thermostat at their apartment. They took the red-headed girl down a

THE LONG SLEEP

row, past some pods that were partly opened. He saw an unmoving hand jutting from one, the nails grown so long they curved down like talons.

Hugo turned and ran. His feet fighting for purchase on the linoleum floor. A nurse shouted behind him, but he ignored her and headed back down the hallway. He tripped on a set of cords and an alarm sounded. His heart stopped, worried that the clawed people would wake and snatch him.

A rough hand pulled him up by the back of his suit. He screamed, but it was only a nurse. The nurse glared at Hugo in disgust and sat him abruptly down on the thin mattress pad of an empty pod.

"Hush. You'll be asleep soon."

"I need my astronaut tape. I'm supposed to have my astronaut tape!"

The nurse nodded at him sternly.

He clamped his mouth shut, embarrassed by the whiny, little-kid strain in his voice. He stared at the nurse's wide nose and the mole that jutted from the man's forehead until the mole started to turn fuzzy and dance off his face.

"There. Just rest. I'll get you hooked up."

Hugo slumped forward and his helmet rolled out of his hands. He moved to pick it up but couldn't reach. Instead, he lay back, too tired to move.

A sharp needle bit into his arm, which he was aware of, but it didn't hurt. His mouth filled with a sour taste like he had taken a swallow from an expired milk carton. He managed to bring his hands up and across his chest as his eyes fluttered, fighting to stay open.

Someone put his helmet at the foot of the pod, in the extra space between his short legs and the edge of the mattress. He could see the blurry shape in between his toes.

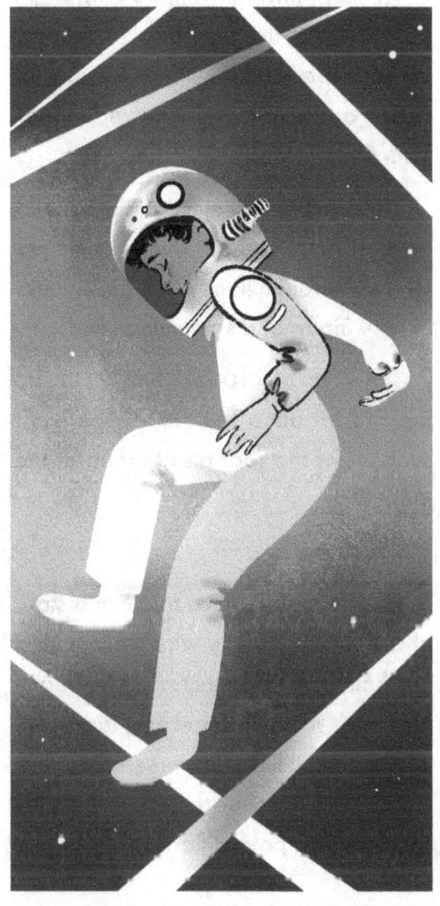

A distant echoey sound came in like whales singing at the bottom of the ocean. He hoped it was Jamie's mix. He closed his eyes and drifted into the long sleep.

He slept through the winter. He slept through the spring and summer. His hair grew long and his skin peeled.

He slept through Jamie's Mars landing. His legs became weak like muscles that have stayed too long in zero-g.

He slept through Jamie's long flight home, where the returning crew conducted experiments in the vacuum of space and examined rare red stones from dry riverbeds.

He slept through elections, urban renewal efforts, and hot humid summers. He slept through heavy rain and chunks of hail. Sirens and screaming winds.

The storm at last woke him. It clawed the old tobacco factory, swiping off sections of the roof and tearing at the old brick.

Hugo's mother once told him a story of a sleeping beauty who woke with a kiss from a handsome prince. He dreamt of Jamie's metallic tinted lips, iridescent and sparkling like stars, pressed against his tingling forehead. Waking up his senses with a painful tickle.

He blinked hard, but sleep clouded his eyes and tinted his vision dark. He prayed to open his eyes to castles and cowboys. Or even better, a Sunday breakfast with both of his parents chomping on bacon and cheesy grits.

He darted his hungry tongue over cracked lips. Dry skin was plastered across his whole body like a thin, fleshy coat. Claws burst out of his fingertips and blunted his touch. His arms and legs were heavy like stones.

Above him, his sight slowly cleared. He saw stars surrounded by a chewy darkness. Water dripped onto his face, making him shiver. He couldn't remember just where he was. He saw himself in a wrecked car, looking out a shattered sunroof—but that couldn't be right. Cold water dripped onto his face, his neck, his shoulders, helping to feel. Must be a hole in the ceiling.

He slowly moved his hands along his body, patting carefully so as not to scratch himself. The lid of his pod had shattered. Wires slid around him like tiny snakes. He levered himself up, breathing hard. He wanted to give up but couldn't. Astronauts don't give up. Even when they're pushing back against hard-g during reentry.

When at last Hugo could stand, he saw the building's red brick ruins

THE LONG SLEEP

surrounded by a filthy moat. Around him, pods lay dark and sealed. The people inside wrapped up tight in hibernation like mummies. The lights on the monitors had gone out.

He called for help, his voice hoarse and duck-like. He could hear the wind still roaring but no sound of anyone else. Not even snoring.

He climbed down from his pallet, limbs still heavy in the wet air. He began to walk, stumbling and crawling at first. Rainwater made ugly puddles on the floor. He shivered and craned his neck to find an exit.

He found he could remember everything he'd heard while dreaming. The distance of the Earth from the sun. The optimal throttle to use when operating asteroid mining equipment. The best of classical pop and electroreggae. He even knew the names of some of the machines connected to the pods. He could add up the increasing costs of hibernation in his head and calculate the rolling wake-up fees that kept so many slumbering. The formulas came to him easily now.

He thought he might build himself a rocket.

He considered the trajectory he'd need to break earth's orbit and rendezvous with the Phobos space station if he left from the observatory in Raleigh, and the fuel he'd need for a Mars heading. He could do whatever he wanted out among the stars. No one can evict you from space. Like Jamie's crewmate, he could watch specially engineered plants soak up the noxious gases of Mars and spit out oxygen.

He wished he had a new memory of how to cut his ugly fingernails. His mother would know. She cared for everyone diligently, making ginger cookies for ill neighbors, listening to Aunt Sarah complain about her job, and waking up early to fix him breakfast. When she came home after working late, she'd sit quietly on the edge of his bed so as not to wake him. He would pretend to be asleep as she whispered a loving goodnight.

Hugo turned his back on the exit and climbed onto the nearest pallet. He pried open the hibernation pod using the emergency release valve. He'd known exactly where it was. Inside, a woman with blonde hair lay sleeping, smelling foul and dusty like a moldy basement. He gagged and reached up to pinch his nose shut. His nails cut a bleeding gash across his face. He cried.

His father told him to pray when he needed courage, and to remember all the people in the past going back forever who were cheering him on from their invisible place in heaven.

Even if he looked like a monster.

He kissed the sleeping woman on her forehead like she was beautiful and tenderly removed all the cords from her body.

He heard Jamie's voice explain the best way to wake a slumbering crew:

"Hibernation is like time travel. The great thing is that we can go really far. The bad news is, you can only ever go in one direction, and that's forward."

One by one, he woke the others from the long sleep and freed them from their debts.

SIM KERN

REAL SUGAR IS HARD TO FIND

Mom's gotten it into her head that we should bake a cake for Nicholle's birthday. "A *real* cake, with butter, milk, and sugar." She's crouched in the mud room, digging through a box of respirators for a set with working cartridges. I've never gotten a real cake for any of my seventeen birthdays, just the Mart-bought kind made of bean flour and corn syrup.

But I've never swallowed a bottle of sleeping pills, either.

Mom shakes out two dusty respirators, the front of the mouthpieces still illuminated by a dim green light. Clearly, it's been months since she's ventured outside our dome. I sneak out all the time, but I never wear a respirator.

I take one, though, slinging it around my neck, because even though my sister is the one who tried to kill herself, it's my mother's emotional fallout that has consumed all my energy this past month.

Nicholle went straight from getting her stomach pumped to a fancy "treatment center" near the lake. I call her once a day and do impressions of Mom to make her laugh. Some part of my brain knows I should be worried about her, but she seems so normal

Mom, on the other hand ... a few days ago, I found her in the pantry, sitting in a puddle of red liquid. Can you imagine how that scared the hell out of me? It was just blackberry wine, though. Holding the bottle had suddenly become too much for her. And then the idea of cleaning it up had been too much for her, so she just sat amid the broken glass and cried. I got her to bed and cleaned up the mess, and that's kind of how the whole month has gone.

So this cake-project is an improvement. Mom is up. Mom is doing stuff, and when she hands me a taser, I pocket it without a snide joke. Mom thinks the world outside the dome is all lawless bands of anarchist punks dying to jump a couple dome-rats for the thrill of it. But it's not like we're going to the Dells, and if we *did* go to the Dells, it's not like a taser would save us.

She climbs into the passenger seat wearing synthetic green work pants with too many pockets, a white solar-block shirt and gloves, broad day hat, and dark-black goggles. They're the kind of clothes you *might* spot on a domeless person, but the fabric is too pristine, and she's still wearing her Silvia Truncheon earrings. Those gold leaves dangling from her earlobes make the whole outfit more like a cringey Halloween costume of a plain-airer than the real deal.

"Stop at the Mart first," she says, buckling her seatbelt. "We can get flour, eggs, and baking powder there."

"So where are we getting this buttermilk-sugar you keep bringing up?"

"Oh, I have my sources."

I snort. "You have *sources*? Outside the dome?"

"Remember those lemon bars Bunmi brought to my last book club?"

"I'm not in your book club."

"But I went on and on about them. I'm sure you remember. Well, turns out she used *real* butter she got from this goat farmer. It's all very hush-hush, though. The mammal ban."

My eyebrows shoot up. Plenty of people in Fox Haven break agriculture laws on the regular. There's a speakeasy outside Waukesha where you can even get real cheeseburgers. But I've never seen Mom buy so much as an extra egg above her weekly ration.

I drive out of our neighborhood and past the coding offices where practically everyone's parents work. Over by the school playground, a scaffold truck is parked against the edge of the dome. Drones scuttle up its hexagonal structure, replacing a panel of thin plastic, riddled with last night's bullet holes.

Mom sucks her teeth.

   REAL SUGAR IS HARD TO FIND

"Seems like they're making replacements every day," she says, pulling the respirator onto her face. "How good can the air be when the dome is a sieve?"

Her voice is metallic now, coming through the respirator's speaker. "Makes you wonder if it's worth what we pay to be on the inside."

Bullshit. She would sell both legs to keep our spot in Fox Haven. But I say nothing, swinging into a parking spot outside the Mart.

Mom has to chat with everyone in the store, bragging about our cake adventure like it's some charming, twentieth-century game, not a ploy to convince her suicidal daughter to go on living. Our neighbors nod and smile, giving her as little encouragement as possible to keep talking. They all know about Nicholle and Dad. So much tragedy for one little family.

By dome standards, it's indecorous, and our neighbors—particularly their kids, shifting their weight next to their parents, checking their Lenses to avoid making eye contact with me—are all desperate to get away from us. But mom is oblivious to the way she grates on others, and it takes fully an hour to get out of there.

By the time we get back In the car, my patience is already threadbare, and we haven't even left the dome. At the western airlock, she tells me to put on my respirator while we're still in the plastic tunnel, but I ignore her.

Guardian drones buzz above the clear-cut land that stretches for half a mile around Fox Haven Dome, their bullets held at bay only by the transmitters embedded in our palms. I don't relax into my seat until they've disappeared around a bend in the road.

"So are you going to tell me where we're going, or am I supposed to drive around until I hit a goat?"

Mom snorts a laugh, then taps the air a few times, and a location appears inside my Lenses. I swipe my hand to send it to the car's nav system but decline the auto-pilot. The roads where we're going will be too full of potholes for the AI to manage. I'm surprised Mom's willing to venture so far from our dome. I've only been to that area once, to this show at The Granary. The bands had all sucked. I'd only gone in hopes of seeing Mahim, but he didn't show up.

The highway out of Fox Haven is lined with skinny, teenage trees. There's a pattern to the foliage—apple, pine, maple, pear—some configuration determined by scientists to maximize food production and carbon reclamation. It repeats at quarter-acre intervals, giving anyone speeding by an unsettling feeling of déjà vu. Dark swoops among the branches could be wild birds or the flying drones that guard the AG company's investments from scavengers.

After a few miles, we hit a patch of younger forest, and the horizon opens up, broken by dozens of glinting domes. But straight ahead is Old Waukesha, which isn't domed. I stop at the first traffic light, where a few people huddle in a bus shelter. A toddler in a stroller tugs on their respirator. Their parent isn't wearing one, nor are the two teenagers leaning their heads together in a way that makes me ache for Mahim.

Mom sinks deeper into her seat, and she taps the passenger panel to arm the car's surface taser.

"Seriously?"

"Sweetie," she sighs. "Do you know how many car jackings there've been here in the last month?"

"No. How many have there been, exactly?" I ask.

She huffs. "Way too many."

"Whatever. You're so domeist. You realize this town is all just, like, families, right? Families trying to get by, do the best for their kids, just like you?"

"Peter, I've lived in this town all my life. I don't need a lecture on it from my own son."

The light turns green, and I pull forward. Main Street is lined with two-story brick buildings, the windows all wrapped in patchwork plastic sheeting to keep out the plain air.

"When my grandmother was a girl, this town was bustling. That was the big theater, where she'd see flat-vids for a quarter. And she always talked about the fountains full of soda."

I've heard this spiel literally every time we've driven through this town since I was five years old. I don't know why, but it makes me want to claw out my own eardrums.

"When I was a girl, though, Waukesha was a ghost town. Everyone had moved out to housing developments, and the stores went bankrupt because people shopped online. But then a few years before you were born, Congress declared the War on Warming. Domed communities were just popping up, and I insisted we buy a house in one.

"Your dad didn't think it was necessary, but good thing we did! Domeless property all got seized and turned over to AG Corps for reforestation, and the domeless had to crowd together in these abandoned downtowns."

She clucks her tongue. "Shame that the architecture is ruined by all that plastic. So much history in these buildings.

     REAL SUGAR IS HARD TO FIND

I wish they could get it together and put a dome over Waukesha."

"It's not that simple, mom. There's no work for them. The system is, like, set up to keep them domeless."

"Oh? And what 'system' is that, exactly?"

I'm not sure how to explain it, but I know I'm right. Mom takes my silence for victory and smiles. I try to remember how Mahim explained it—something about the racist-classist-domeist praxis. But thinking about Mahim makes my heart lurch, and my mind go gooey, and all I can remember is kissing him that night at the Gorge, when we stayed up talking until the sun rose out of the lake.

My stomach wrenches, and for the millionth time, I regret not asking for his Handle. We could've been chatting on our Lenses this whole month, but I was worried about looking too eager. I'd said, "See you around," and I was sure I would—at the next silo show or abandoned-mall rave. But he'd disappeared from the scene, and now I had no way of talking to the one person in the world whose presence didn't make me feel more alone.

In a town called Milford, the car's nav system sends me north down a farm-to-market road lined with soybean fields. For twenty miles, massive harvester drones are the only breaks between us and the horizon. Finally, an old industrial mill looms up ahead. I pull onto a dirt lot beneath the towering grain cylinders, surrounded by low buildings made of aluminum siding.

"How do you know this is safe?" I ask.

"Weren't you the one saying everywhere is just families? Who's being domeist now?" She taps her mask. "Put it on."

But I leave the respirator around my neck as I get down to help her out of the car. A short, gray-haired woman crosses the gravel parking lot, calling to someone behind her in a south Asian language.

"Hello!" Mom begins, speaking too loudly. "We," she points to me and her, "are looking," she shades her eyes with her hand, "for … dairy." She hesitates, then mimes milking a cow.

"My son will be out to help you in a moment," the woman says, with only a trace of an accent. I stare at the ground, willing it to open and swallow me whole, so I don't see her son approaching.

"So, like, how can I help you?"

Our eyes meet, and I can't seem to breathe, because it's him. The guy I've been losing sleep over all month. The guy with the black hair that falls into his eyes and those impossibly soft lips.

My heart swells with excitement, but only for an instant. Then it's dropping out of my body and into the depths of hell, as I realize that Mom is here next to me, shouting through her respirator at the man-of-my-dreams, Mahim.

"We're looking for milk?" She mimes spreading something on bread. "And butter?"

Mahim smiles at me. "She's not a cop?"

"I mean," I gesture at the ridiculous woman. "Does she seem like it?"

He laughs once and says something to his mother in their language, then waves for us to follow. I am tripping over my feet for staring at the divot in the back of his neck and the broad plains of his shoulders. As he leads us through a labyrinth of homemade buildings, I rip my respirator off my neck and try to shove it in my back pocket, but it won't fit, so I just sling it back on, where it thumps against my chest with each step, like it's saying, *dome boy, dome boy, dome boy.*

That night at the Gorge, I told Mahim everything about myself, save one. When I venture outside Fox Haven, I never cop to where I'm from. I don't belong there, with those lemon-bar-people. I belong in the plain air, with carbon particulate in my lungs and a heart full of loss.

Mahim leads us into a pasture, shaded by a lattice of brightly colored plastic strips. The screening still lets in plenty of sunlight, and a dozen goats are happily munching on tall grass.

"How do y'all keep all this hush-hush?" Mom asks conspiratorially. "Isn't mammal farming illegal?"

I cringe. Her old-timey southern drawl always gets worse around strangers. Her mother was from Tennessee but moved north after the burning of Appalachia. That was years before Mom was born, so her accent is totally fake—picked up from old flatvids.

"The screening keeps drones from picking out the livestock," Mahim gestures overhead. "And grandma has me vet who we sell to. I'm *usually* pretty good at reading folks." He knits his eyebrows in my direction, and I can't tell if it's a flirty look or if he's disappointed that I turned out to be a dome-rat.

Mom notices the exchange and, to my horror, tries to help. "You know, you boys look about the same age! What are you? 16?"

"17."

"Exactly the same! You should exchange Handles."

"Mom, drop it," I hiss, guts churning miserably. Of course, I've been working up the courage to ask Mahim for his Handle, but now it's going to look like I'm some loser whose mommy has to help him score dates.

Mom and I shoot eye-daggers at each other until Mahim suggests we head into the old mill. Inside, I'm hit by that animal stink again. Stalls line one wall, and on the other are refrigerators and long rows of tables covered in fabric-wrapped cheese.

"How much are you looking to buy?" Mahim asks.

"Well, the cake recipe calls for a half cup of butter and a half cup of milk..."

"But you want extra, right?" he says. "What if the cake doesn't work on your first try?"

I raise my eyebrows. *You slick salesman, you.* He smiles back. Maybe he doesn't loathe me completely. Maybe I can salvage this.

"Good thinking," Mom says. "Let's double it, then. I could always try baking Bunmi's lemon bars."

"You could bake lots of things," he says. "And butter lasts in the fridge six months."

"No kidding?" Mom clasps her hands under her chin. "Okay, you've sold me. We'll take five pounds of butter and two gallons of milk."

An expression of surprise flits across Mahim's face, and my guts churn. It's too much. As he pulls blocks of butter from an ice chest, I realize Mom never even asked what it would cost. I see us through his eyes—a couple dome-rats spending a small fortune to bake sweets. Repulsive.

I carry the jugs of milk while he totes bricks of cloth-wrapped butter back to the car. Mom chatters the whole way, every word a nail in my reputation's coffin.

"You were so helpful today, May-heem! Why don't you two exchange Handles? You know, Petey got a perfect score on the math section of his pre-C-Cat? Maybe you guys could study together?"

"Stop it, Mom. He doesn't care," I whisper.

"And I'm sure you could help Peter with the, uh...agricultural section—is there an agricultural section to the C-Cat?"

"I'm not really sure—" Mahim starts.

"There's not," I say.

"Petey's looking at mostly in-state colleges. Not that he can't get into an out-of-state school. But Madison is fully domed, and every bit as good as the Ivies. Is Madison a good AG school? Or there I go, assuming. Maybe you're thinking of majoring in something else."

I heave the jugs of milk into the backseat. "He's probably not going to college at all?" I blurt, too angrily.

"Well, that's quite an assumption," Mom says.

"Yeah, Petey," Mahim says quietly, "That's quite an assumption." He places the blocks of butter next to the milk.

My face is on fire. "I'm sorry—I didn't mean—"

"No, you're right," he says. "I'm not going to college. I'm just a fucking dome-less, right? Probably gonna milk goats forever."

"I might not go either ... I don't care about that shit anyways."

"Sure, *perfect score*."

He swipes a hand to send Mom the bill, which causes her face to pucker in shock. Whatever it costs, she pays it without protest. Mahim won't meet my eyes.

"Thanks for your business," he says to Mom. "Come back anytime."

And then he's walking away, hands in his pockets, cool and lean and lost to me forever. Mom purses her lips, shakes her head at me, and climbs up into the passenger seat.

"Now getting the sugar, that's going to be the real trick. A pound of cane sugar was a dollar when I was a girl. A dollar! Of course, you can't get cane sugar now. I don't think there's anywhere left it'll grow. And beet sugar—well they used to grow beets around here, but not for decades past. The nights just don't get cold enough. I hear they're still growing beets up in Canada, but I haven't seen sugar at the Mart for years."

I'm not paying attention. I'm busy reliving those last moments with Mahim, imagining a million different things I could have said that wouldn't have ruined things. I'm also not paying atten-tion to where we're going, how it's north-west, northwest, northwest, until deep inside an old-growth forest, we pass the smoking wreckage of a police drone on the side of the road.

Then it hits me: what's northwest, nor-thwest, northwest of Waukesha.

I pull up the nav app and zoom in on the address Mom gave me. A river, a lake, a wide swath of green.

"We can't go here!" I slam on the brakes, pulling off the road. "This is in the Dells."

"What? No, that can't be right." Mom pulls up the address on her passenger panel. "Look, there's the Dells. This is right *outside* the Dells."

"Where did you get this address? There's no way Bunmi came here."

"I—I saw an ad for a flea market."

"Where?"

"In an email."

"Show me."

Mom swipes her hand. An envelope appears in the corner of my lenses, and I flick my wrist to open it.

Pop-up Flea Market! Rare food-stuffs and goods!

- *Freon canisters*
- *Virgin Cotton*
- *Granulated Sugar*

I check the message's subdata. "Mom this IP is from an unregistered server. It's dome-rat bait. They're luring you in to rob you."

"That can't be right. It didn't trip my scam filter."

"Well your scam filter fucking sucks!"

Mom's eyes go wide, and I instantly regret the curse word. Swearing just shuts her down, making communication impossible. She flings open the door and climbs out of the SUV. I cut the engine and hop down after her.

"Mom, I'm sorry about cursing, but you need to get back in the car."

She's power-walking up the road, gazing straight ahead like she can't hear me.

"Mom, there's a blown-up police drone *right there*. This is Dells' territory. They are going to *rob* us and probably kill us."

"I thought everywhere was *just families*," she mimics.

"Gahhh!" I claw my hands down my face. "Most places are, but this is the most dangerous place in Wisconsin!"

"You want to know what's dangerous?" Mom rounds on me and flicks the mask resting on my chest. "What? You're too cool to wear it? I can't understand you, Peter. Don't you ever think of your father?"

"Dad *never* wore a respirator outside."

"*Exactly!*" she screams, voice flying into a shriek, the speakers on her respirator maxing out. Her eyes are wide and wet with grief. "You want to be a risk-taker like your dad? Oh, he was so *cool*. Well, maybe your mom feels like taking some risks today!" She brushes past me and marches up the road. "We can't go back without the sugar."

"Of course we can!" I shake my pressed palms together, literally begging as I chase her up the road. "We can get a Mart cake! Nicholle wouldn't want us to get killed—"

Then we freeze, hearing it in the same moment—a growling out of another century. Somewhere to the north, a diesel engine roars towards us, choking and sputtering on fossil fuels. Mom touches my wrist, and at last I see common sense dawning in her eyes. We make for the SUV, but Mom is not a fast runner.

A black truck on monster wheels speeds around the curve behind us. I take Mom's arm to usher her faster, but the truck speeds to a stop before us, cutting off our path. A thunderous bass line pulses from the cab, like the beating of a monster's heart.

It goes silent, and the driver's window slides slowly into its frame.

The driver could be my age, but with strung-out eyes and the pockmarked skin of an addict. They lean one arm out of the cab, real casually. There's a gun in their hand.

Mom's taser hangs heavy and useless in my pocket.

"What brings a couple of fine folks like you to the Dells?"

Mom's oblivious act is so convincing, I actually believe she thinks "these nice young men" are giving us a ride to the "flea market," even as they confiscate our tasers and usher us up into the back of the truck. They take the road north, of course, towards the Dells, the old country-club-turned-crime-syndicate. My terror is a ringing in my ears and a heaviness in my limbs that makes me docile and obedient. But Mom is chatty.

Mom comments on the beauty of Mirror Lake and the golf course-turned-prairie, and the pretty architecture of the old clubhouse, despite its windows wrapped in plastic, its bricks streaked with acid rain. She smiles as they lead us into the gutted building and down a stairwell to the basement.

But as soon as we hear the *ka-chunk* of the bolt lock in the door, Mom collapses to the damp cement and chucks her respirator across the cement floor.

She sobs into her arms.

"It's okay," I say, getting down on my knees beside her.

I rub her back, and it's such a familiar role that I get a weird feeling of déjà vu. I realize that it doesn't matter whether we're home on a pleasant afternoon in Fox Haven or waiting on execution in the basement of a notorious gang hideout—I'll still, always, be the one rubbing Mom's back.

The thought makes a little of the fear ebb from my bloodstream. A little anger rushes in.

"Get it together, Mom."

She sobs harder.

"I mean it. You should be comforting *me*. You're the parent here, for fuck's sake!"

She doesn't even seem to hear the curse word.

Disgusted, I swipe a few times to try the police, but there's no signal. Even if

     REAL SUGAR IS HARD TO FIND

I got through, everyone knows cops won't go near the Dells.

The cement floor is patterned in rust-colored stains that I'm trying not to think about. There's a pile of mildewed upholstered chairs, and high on the opposite wall is a narrow window. I drag one of the chairs over and climb up. The glass is thick and spiderwebbed with metal mesh. I look around for something sturdy enough to break it. Hell if I'm going to die down here—not before I ever fall in love, or have sex, or at least try apologizing to Mahim.

The lock *ka-chunks* again.

Mom lifts her head, and I ease back down to the floor.

A man walks in—and, okay, I assume he's a man, because he's of my mother's generation, without a wisp of femininity about him. He has sun-leathered skin and wears white shirtsleeves cuffed to his forearms, and there's something out-of-time about his sturdiness. Like he's composed entirely of mammal meat and grain alcohol. There's a coldness in his eyes and a firmness of his jaw that makes me certain he's never smiled for anyone else's comfort.

"We were ... looking for the flea market?" Mom says. She looks fragile as a porcelain tchotchke, still kneeling at his feet. The man turns those hard eyes down to her, and she straightens her spine. "We were hoping to buy some sugar? To bake a cake for my daughter—"

How can she still be thinking about cake? I turn to the man, keeping my eyes low. "We are so sorry for interrupting your, uh, operation," I say. "My mom's not great with directions—"

"Don't interrupt your elders." His voice sends a shock of fear straight to my bladder.

"Thank you," Mom breathes. "Like I was saying, my daughter, she—well, about a month ago, she tried—" Her voice cracks.

"Mom, he doesn't care about Nicholle. Let's just—"

Both their heads whip towards me, and I fall silent.

"Nicholle had an incident. With my sleeping pills." She fiddles with a stuck zipper on one of her pants' cargo pockets. "She wrote this—" The zipper tugs free, and she pulls out a folded square of notebook paper.

My gut roils with betrayal. "You never told me Nicholle left a note."

"A poem." Mom's hands shake as she unfolds the paper.

"You're not gonna read it? Mom, he doesn't care—"

"How many times do I have to tell you to shut up?" the man growls.

I mime zipping my lips and I clench my jaw, feeling like I've fallen through my own Lenses into a surreal holovid. The crimelord of the Dells wants to hear my sister's suicide-poem? Sure. Why the hell not?

Mom clears her throat and reads, in her most high-falluting, antebellum drawl.

"*The only monkeys I'll ever know lived in the print on dad's shirt—* that was my husband," she adds. "He passed last year from lung cancer."

The man nods. As Mom reads on, I picture Nicholle here in the basement, conjured by her own words. Her lank hair hangs down, paper notebook clutched to her chest. All our schoolwork is done on-Lenses, so it annoys people, that pretension with the real paper. I've tried to teach her to be cooler, but she has no instinct for it.

Everything is getting terrible.
The deserts creep north.
We bite fleas as if they were delicacies,
Eyeing the dragon on the side of the road.

Oh Nicholle, why can't you just say what you mean? Or at least rhyme. By "fleas," does she mean cricket-cakes? She's been vegetarian the last few years, refusing to eat even insects. And what's this dragon about? An AG drone?

Then I realize what I'm doing. Criticizing her suicide poem. My eyes burn, and I swear I'll never tease her again. I'll read all her poems and memorize every last sentimental word, because it's truly fucking hitting me. Something about hearing Mom read her poem—in this probably torture-basement in the Dells, to the weirdly rapt attention of Wisconsin's most dangerous man—makes it all crushingly real for the first time. We almost lost her.

The twin arbors have fallen and there is no silver behind the walls.
Sweetness went extinct,
long before I was born.
There's no real pleasure in life.

Mom falls silent, her cheeks as wet with tears as mine. She refolds the letter with trembling hands. "Her birthday's on Friday, and that line—*sweetness went extinct*—it got me thinking about cakes my mother made when I was little. And then I got this email ..."

"Those emails are dome-rat bait," the man says.

"Peter tried to tell me," Mom nods. "Oh, please don't hurt him. Oh, I can't stand for anything bad to happen to my children." She buries her face in her hands and cries.

The man squats down to her level. "I had a niece, who was mentally ... upset."

      REAL SUGAR IS HARD TO FIND

Mom looks up.

"She went through with it."

Mom holds a hand to her mouth. "I'm so sorry."

They hold each other's gazes, and with a sickening lurch, I realize what is going on here. I have to choke down revulsion, because it is so gross, that they are bonding over teen girl suicides and looking at each other like—well, like me and Mahim looked at each other a few hours ago.

Then I remember how easily I'd shattered that connection, and I'm praying to all the gods of history that Mom will keep her foot out of her mouth long enough for this horny old gangster to let us go.

"Here's what's going to happen," he says. "I'm taking your car and whatever's in your bank account." He spreads his hands wide. "I'm a businessman, and I've got people to take care of. I'm trying to get us our own dome here."

Mom sniffles, nodding.

"But we did just get in a shipment of sugar. And I could go for a slice of cake."

We're given the use of the big industrial kitchen, and the help of Shie, a burly woman with sharp-cornered eyes and fox-ear implants. Stew is more her specialty, she admits, but she bangs open dust-filled cabinets until she finds us a set of cake pans. We go with her to grab ingredients from the "pantry"— an old ballroom that's set up like a Mart, only aside from the standard groceries, it's stocked with sugar and tropical plants and packets of drugs, and long, black guns.

As Mom measures out ingredients, adrenaline leeches from my bones. I'm suddenly so tired, I want to pass out for a week in one of the kitchen's steel cabinets. But when Mom tells me to stir a bowl of gloop, I stir. I'm sure we've done something wrong, because the gloop doesn't look anything like cake.

But we watch through the oven door as the cakes balloon up, like magic. Two barefoot kids run into the kitchen asking for a snack. Shie scoops up a kid that looks like her and sets them on her hip. She lets the kids swipe their tiny fingers around the inside of the mixing bowl, until every speck of batter is licked clean.

The kids run out the back door to play down by the lakeshore, and Shie follows, hollering at them not to get any water in their mouths.

In the moment of privacy, I catch Mom's eye. "See?" I say. "Just families."

She laughs and whacks me playfully on the sternum.

I whisk butter and sugar together for the icing, forcing my voice to stay even. "Why didn't you tell me about the poem?"

Mom frowns at the cooling cakes.

"Because everything in it was true. It's been messing with my head, and I just ... I wanted to protect you from that. Like her sadness could infect you or something."

"You think I'm not aware? You think I don't freak out about the dying of the world?"

Mom makes a sound that's half-laugh and half-sob, and the old urge to comfort her rushes in.

"Look, everything in that poem wasn't true. *Sweetness is extinct?* This icing tastes pretty fucking sweet to me."

Mom narrows her eyes at me for the curse word, but her lips tighten in a smile. She swipes a finger in the bowl, licks it, and moans with pleasure.

When the cakes are cooled and stacked, we do our best to smooth the white buttercream over them. Shie finds some food coloring in the way back of a cabinet, left over from when the place was still a country club.

I try writing 'Happy Birthday Nicholle!' in blue icing, but the letters come out so crooked, we turn them into fluffy blue clouds on a white background. Like an inverse image of the sky.

I hold the cake in my lap, hoping the roaring engine won't shake it to pieces. Shie sits up front with Torrin—that's the guy who picked us up off the farm-to-market road. Allen, the gangster-looking dude, follows behind us in a car that's really more of a tank.

We blast through old Waukesha. Bystanders whip their heads to track us, then recoil when they spot the circle-D spray-painted on the vehicles' doors. We zoom past a police patrol-drone that only manages half a whoop of its siren before a mortar turns it to a pile of smoking rubble in the rearview mirror. Torrin cheers.

Then we are speeding downhill towards the biggest dome I've ever seen, framed by the glittering blue expanse of Lake Michigan. I'm hit by a cascade of memories—all those camping trips we took with Dad, before he got sick. Sneaking off to watch the sunrise with him and Nicholle, before Mom got up and nagged us into wearing our respirators. When this is all over, I'm going to take Nicholle camping again. I'll fix her hair and take her to parties at the Granary, and we will dance to bad music beneath the plain, poisoned sky.

I expect Torrin to slow down as we approach the no-man's land outside

REAL SUGAR IS HARD TO FIND

Calming Dunes Treatment Center, but he accelerates instead. The barrels of the drones' guns swivel to track us, and the breath goes out of my lungs. Torrin swipes a hand, activating something.

And they drop. All the dozens of drones in sight drop to the earth. He and Shie cackle with laughter. I am struggling to suck in a lungful of air.

"Well, would you look at that," Mom says, and I assume she means whatever happened with the drones. But then I see that her eyes are clouded-over.

She swipes something off her Lenses. "Allen left $10,000 in the bank account. That'll be enough for groceries until my next paycheck, and we can keep Nicholle in treatment until the end of the month. What a nice man!"

Shie and I make the same baffled snort simultaneously. "Did you forget he just robbed you?" She turns in her seat. "He's my dad, you know."

Torrin pulls into the Calming Dunes airlock. He rolls the window down slow and hangs his arm out the window, tapping his gun against the door. The guard in the booth holds up both hands, and the inner airlock slides open.

Slowly, we rumble up a long, shaded drive. Grazing deer look up as we pull up into a courtyard lined with long brick dormitories. Dozens of people in white pajamas are streaming out of the doors to gawk at us, while a few people in suits try in vain to usher them back inside.

The engines fall silent, and we climb down. Torrin and the guys who rode with Allen hang back, leaning against the monster truck tires and vaping something that smells like burnt plastic.

I step forward, balancing a tower made of butter, milk, and sugar on my palms. Shie follows at my side, scratching a furry ear with the silver cake cutter, and Allen takes my mother's arm, like they're a couple from an old flatvid.

Across a lawn dotted with bunny rabbits, my sister's notebook drops to her side. Her eyes fill with so many questions, until they find mine. And see the cake. And then her smile is huge with real delight.

LAURA BARKER

MA DRESDEN

Ma Dresden is tall. Let's start there. She's taller than I am, she's taller than the rest of our family, and she has tall legs as well. She never has to get on her tiptoes to reach anything, not in her own house, not in anyone else's. She hasn't stood on her tiptoes for years. Her left leg is slightly taller than her right leg. And she has locs down to her knees, white with age at the top, and black with youth at the bottom. A living archive. It's quite striking. But you'd never really notice Ma Dresden's hair because of the eyes.

I know all this even though my seeing days are well behind me. No, do not feel sorry for me. Not being able to see properly anymore is the least of my worries, and I mean that very literally. But I know that you want a visual description, so that's what I'm going to give you.

She has a face like a milk bun. Because Ma Dresden has a face like a milk bun, you don't realize at first that she's got these eyes. You think she's got a lovely warm face, and then you look up those rich fat soft cheeks and you feel happy inside until you catch a glimpse of the eyes and you have to button your coat up right to the neck, right that instant. That's how chilling these eyes are. And

I'm someone who hates buttoning up their coat right up to the neck.

Oh, you can speculate about why, if you like, but if you really want to know, you can ask my mother. She still lives at 28 Twobuckle Street and she'll be alive for another ten years, guaranteed. And don't go feeling sorry for me because when you're on different sides of a war, even a silent, static, not going anywhere war like this one, when you come up on each other, you have to fight each other, especially if there's someone watching, which there was.

I was lucky to get away with the thick scars around my neck and a lifelong aversion to people getting too close to my throat or kissing me from behind. It's not all bad. I've sort of switched roles. Now I do all the kissing from behind and the other person simpers into my arms. You just have to adjust to a new kind of life.

Anyway. You didn't come here to learn about my neck. You came to learn about Ma Dresden's eyes. So here it is.

Snake eyes, people call it. That's what it's called in a casino when you roll two dice and they both come up showing the single digit meaning one. It's a 2.77% chance that you'll throw two ones, the same chance of throwing two of anything, but throwing snake eyes is supposedly bad luck.

What people always want to know is if she can still see through them, and the answer is yes. They're regular eyes, for all intents and purposes, but the iris is white so the pupil is just a round dot in an otherwise completely white eye. The medically minded of you are thinking of arcus selinis, where phospholipid and cholesterol collect in the cornea and sometimes cover the iris in white patches. No. We are talking about an iris that has no outer ring around it. It is not pale, it is not faded, it is completely white. You can't see it at all.

The politically correct of you are thinking, "Fine. What does it matter if her eyes don't look like conventional eyes? I would treat her just the same anyway."

Ha! You have no idea what you're talking about. Yes, there is a whole generation of us whose bodies have been ruined by this silent and violent war, but this isn't that. Those eyes are not a disfigurement. They are a consequence of what Ma Dresden has done.

This is how it happened. Ma Dresden walks into a bar. This sounds like the beginning of a joke, but believe me it's not funny. Some people laugh when they hear about it, but it's a shock laugh, not a real laugh. Ma Dresden walks into a bar. She meets a man. Nothing untoward, she's happily married and he's happily widowed, but they talk for a while.

When Ma Dresden walks out several hours' later, she's carrying a suitcase. That suitcase is full of money. She takes it home.

Now, she doesn't go wild with it. The next day she treats herself to breakfast out. She goes to her nearest greasy spoon and says, "A four please," which on this menu means a full vegetarian breakfast. In this particular greasy spoon, a full vegetarian breakfast is the works. Fried bread, fried bubble (and squeak), fried vegetarian sausage, fried egg, baked beans, fried onions, mushrooms from a can reheated on the same heated disc they put the bacon on, which improves the flavour no end, hash browns, two grilled tomatoes, a tea, and your choice of salad or chips. She chooses chips, of course, because she's no idiot. You don't go to a greasy spoon for a salad.

So to be clear, it's a pretty full breakfast, but it is in no way a splurge compared to what she could have bought with that money. So she's being sensible. She eats her breakfast, she relaxes for a while, has another cup of sweet milky tea, reads the free papers the proprietor's got out on the counter, chats to a few other customers—a truck driver from Luton, a woman who is recently bereaved and can only stomach black coffee—and she gets home.

Her husband is waiting for her inside the house. He's holding the suitcase. Now, she didn't think he'd ever find it because she put it in the cupboard under the stairs where she keeps the vacuum cleaner and the mop and all the cleaning products. That was her little joke. The one place he wouldn't look because the man has never cleaned the house.

When I say she's happily married, I mean she's happy to be married because she likes the institution. She does not like her husband. She thinks he's an idiot. But when he asks her what's going on, she tells him the truth. She's not much of a liar. She only does it occasionally, around the edges, to soften things that would otherwise be too painful to hear. But not with the big stuff. So she tells him that she met a man in a bar who was trying to get rid of it.

Her husband says there's no such thing as a free lunch. This really gets her, so she says, "That's funny because I've been making you lunch these past fifty years and I don't see me getting paid for it."

He says they have a division of labour. He takes care of things outside the house, she takes care of things inside the house. What he means is, she works from home. She's a hairdresser, a loctician to be specific, and she works from their living room. She earns as much as him—more, some months, and besides, she is the one that takes care of all the finances. He would spend it all on luxury garden tools if he had his way.

They have an almighty row. She threatens to leave him. He threatens to go to the police about the suitcase of money. Now things are really starting to heat up. She laughs in his face.

"I'll go to the police about how you cut me," she says.

"How I what?" he says.

But already she's picked up a knife and she's dragged it down her forearm and she's bleeding. She puts the knife into his hand and at first he's too shocked to drop it.

But then he does drop it. She smiles, thinking she's won. He gets up. He says, "A man that would cut you would have no problem smashing all your grand-mother's crockery."

Now this crockery has been a bone of contention between them since they got married. He wants to use it on special occasions. She has seen no occasion special enough to use it. She's kept it pristine in the box all these years. He's not even allowed to touch it. And now he gets it down in its box and he doesn't even open the box, he just jumps on it, up and down, up and down, smash, smash, smash.

It's all coming out now. She stands on the spot, opens her mouth, and screams. Then she squirts hot sauce in his eye, he throws washing up liquid in her hair, there are vegetables everywhere, and one of them, they're not even sure which one, lets the dog out of the front door.

"Who's going to clean this mess up?" she's shouting. And he's saying that with all her new money, she could hire all the cleaners in the world.

Which is what she does. She makes sure the house is filthy first, to make it worth it. She's smashing all kinds of things—all the remaining crockery, his glasses, bottles of wine that he's been saving. He's squirting mayonnaise on the furniture and spraying the dog's pheromones they got to calm him down on Bonfire Night all over the kitchen windows and all over the floor. She makes a call to a cleaning company that deals with forensic mishaps, and they both leave the house. They come back to it spotless.

They call a truce. He thinks it's real. He's happy they've released a bit of tension. He thinks they can go back to normal. Better than normal. He thinks this has been good for them. That night he turns over to her and puts a hand on her arm and suggests they have a little sexual intercourse. She laughs so loud he can feel his eardrums hurting.

She is bubbling with an intense rage that has been building for a long time. The whole of their marriage has been leading to this point. She realises that this is why they were brought together like this, so she can become her most powerful self and do away with him once and for all.

She waits until he's fallen asleep and she creeps out of the house. It's way past curfew time and the authorities have the power to fine you on the spot and levitate you if they catch you, but she knows their patterns and they won't come to Two-buckle Street for another hour at least.

The good thing about the curfew is you know any establishment open after hours is up to no good. That's the kind of certainty you need when you're up to no good yourself. There are candles lit at the local medicine woman's. Ma Dresden leaves an offering of oil on the stoop and rings the bell.

MA DRESDEN

Mama Levi comes to the door. "What the fresh hell is wrong with you," she says, "Ringing my doorbell like the filth."

Ma Dresden apologises. She's on edge. She's never done this before, she doesn't know how it's done, but Mama Levi can see what's going on and she pulls out a chair and draws Ma Dresden a lilac wine. "Speak," she says.

Ma Dresden explains what she wants. Mama Levi says the same thing she says to anyone who comes to her about curses, "What are you willing to lose?"

Ma Dresden tells her she has plenty of money right now. Mama Levi laughs. Not a real laugh. A laugh to indicate Ma Dresden's stupidity.

"No, my dear," she says. "Money is only an appropriate sacrifice when it comes from someone who has barely any of it. Not saying I won't take some, mind. I will. But Mother Earth is cruel. She will want something from you that will really hurt. So I ask again. What are you willing to lose?"

Ma Dresden thinks about it. She comes up with a number of things that let Mama Levi know that she's serious—or she thinks she's serious, which amounts to the same thing.

They settle on her irises. Or the black of her eyes, as Mama Levi calls them. Ma Dresden is no longer a young woman,

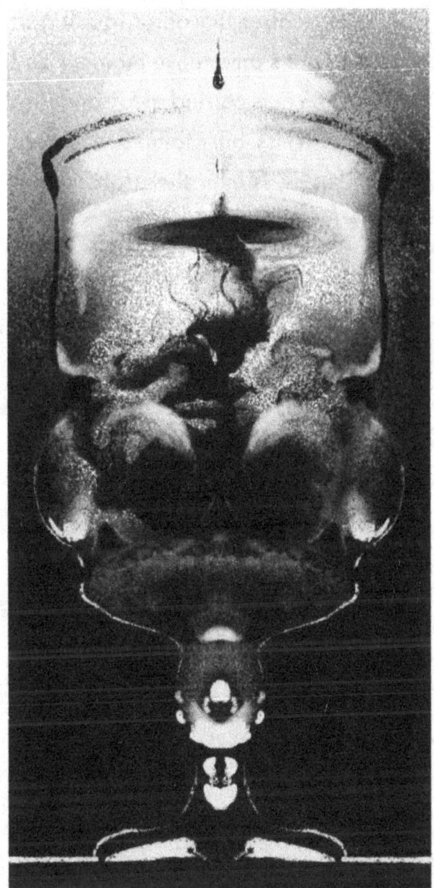

but even in this society that worships youth, her eyes are cherished, doted on by men young and old. People still cross the street to tell her how beautiful they are. A most appropriate sacrifice, Mama Levi thinks.

Money is exchanged. Ma Dresden scratches the cut she made earlier on her forearm and Mama Levi pierces the tip of her finger with a glucose tester. They let their blood fall into the same fresh cup of lilac wine and both of them drink from it, one after the other, gazing at each other. It's an intense moment and Ma Dresden gets carried away and tries to go in for a kiss, but Mama Levi, moved though she is, is ever the professional, and she pushes her away.

"None of that," she says, "I just ate."

Ma Dresden gets home and crawls into bed beside her husband. Soon she is astride him, and he is happy, believing his wife loves him and merely wanted to make it seem like the sexual intercourse was her idea. He does not notice that she was ever away. They fall back asleep naked.

The next morning he makes her breakfast for the very first time ever, orange juice freshly squeezed, and she wonders if she made the wrong decision. She rings Mama Levi.

"It's too late for that now," says Mama Levi, and Ma Dresden does what she has always done, and makes herself believe she has chosen what is coming next.

At lunchtime, she looks at herself in the mirror. When her irises disappear leaving her two white marbles with dilating black dots in their centres, she knows it is done. She goes downstairs and looks at the plate on the table. She can tell it is him, even though he looks every bit the part—rice made from his bones, meat of his flesh, and gravy which is his blood. The vegetables are actual bona fide vegetables because she does not like to take a meal without greens.

She wonders at first whether she can eat her husband. Then she remembers him threatening to call the police about the money—her money—and she presses his meat to her mouth. It is delicious. Soft, tender, salty. The most expensive meal she has ever eaten. It would be an insult to her husband's memory not to enjoy it.

LINDSAY KING-MILLER

AN EVENTUAL FEAST

Aisha Greer had been dead three weeks when she followed Zophie to the door of our family compartment. Zophie's face was gray and nervous on the peephole monitor, her right eyebrow twitching just slightly. I opened the door and she hurried through, yanking it shut behind her as though Aisha might try to follow. She didn't, though; she seemed content to wait in the hall.

The dead always seemed content to wait. They knew we would be joining them soon enough.

"It's been at my heels for three days," said Zophie, in answer to the question I didn't want to ask. She pitched her voice low enough that Ave, in the next room, couldn't hear her. I suppose it was a reflex developed through her decades of birth work, to keep her personal troubles from unsettling her patient.

"Christ," I said helplessly. "I'm sorry." Zophie was clearly terrified, the lines on her face drawn tight and sharp. I ached for her, but mixed with my pity was fear of my own.

If Zophie died—and Aisha's presence outside proclaimed she soon would—who would deliver Ave's baby? We were on a spaceship with a population of six hundred people, and exactly one of them was a midwife.

Zophie pressed the heels of her hands against her eye sockets, as though to staunch tears, but when she looked back at me her eyes were dry. "Let's go see how your spouse is doing."

Back on Earth, we would have figured out why it was happening. We might have even found a way to stop it. There would have been public health funding, state-of-the-art laboratories, big-name researchers and young upstart scientists trying to make their name deciphering how the dead rose and walked.

But aboard the Ark, with our home planet two years behind us and our destination—if we had one—generations in the future, we didn't have the time, resources, or personnel to spare, not for a non-essential question. Oxygen, water, food, medicine: if something didn't directly threaten those vital supplies, it was a secondary concern.

Some of us called them zombies, of course—we'd lived on Earth most of our lives, we'd seen movies—but they weren't exactly like their Hollywood namesakes. They weren't grayish or decaying, for one thing. They looked like perfect replicas of their living selves sculpted from some kind of poisonously green moss, and their faces or bodies squirmed, as though things were moving just below the skin.

For another, they didn't eat the living. They merely followed us around, waiting for us to die. Only then did they devour us.

Zophie and I walked through the front room (which the Ark's schematics anachronistically labeled a "parlor") and into the bedroom, where Ave was sitting up in bed, typing.

They were a theoretical botanist, part of the team that oversaw the gardens, greenhouses, and air filtration systems. One of their long-term projects, discussed and then back-burnered every month like clockwork, was to "investigate anomalies in the human remains composting process"—that is, figure out why we had zombies. Although Ave was ostensibly on pregnancy leave since the beginning of the third trimester, they still worked as much as they ever had, albeit with a longer midday break for naps.

"Hey, Zoph. Hey, Magda," they said without looking up. "Is it nine already?"

I bent over and kissed the top of their head, where their hair swirled in a perfect cowlick. "Just about," I said.

Actually, Zophie was a few minutes early. Maybe she'd been awake before

   AN EVENTUAL FEAST

her alarm this morning, listening for Aisha in the dark.

Of course, the dead don't breathe, but if it's quiet enough you can hear a sort of low hum in their vicinity. It's not a human sound; it doesn't come from their vocal cords, but from the green stuff, the algae and microorganisms. That genetically engineered soup that was supposed to digest dead bodies into clean soil and water but instead made them get up and walk.

Ave tapped a sequence of buttons on their computer, and it shut down and retracted into the wall. I stood awkwardly in the doorway while Zophie checked Ave's blood pressure and the fetus's position. I always felt ancillary during these prenatal visits, unsure what I could contribute as the non-gestational mother. Now, the knowledge that Aisha waited outside our door made me even more fidgety and distracted than usual.

With Zophie's help, Ave got to their feet and slipped into the bathroom to provide a urine sample. Normally, in their absence, Zophie would turn to me and ask how I was doing, perhaps suggest a new breathing exercise or herbal tincture for my anxiety. "I'm not just Ave's midwife, I'm your family's midwife," she'd reminded me more than once. "It's my job to take care of all of you."

Sometimes we'd talk about how I could help during the birth; sometimes I'd just take the space to acknowledge, outside of Ave's hearing, the terror that always shimmered at the corners of my vision. There had never yet been a baby born in space. Two years into this voyage, we were over the edge of the map, where nameless monsters roamed. Nobody really knew how this would go.

Usually Zophie calmed my nerves. She'd remind me that she was extensively trained, had attended hundreds of births back on Earth, and besides, we had a team of surgeons and every conceivable medical technology at our disposal. The Ark was short on luxuries and living space, but no expense had been spared on the possibility of producing future generations of humanity.

But today she had no words of reassurance to offer me. We stood in the tiny room avoiding each other's eyes.

"Maybe it's nothing," I said finally, just to be saying something.

"It's not nothing," she said. I couldn't respond to that, because I knew she was right.

Somehow, the dead could predict death. The green stuff they were made of was designed to quickly digest human remains into materials that could be fed back into our greenhouses and food supply, but instead of waiting for bodies to come to them in the composting facility, they climbed out of their slime vats and went foraging. When they began to follow a living Ark passenger around, it was a sign that person would die soon—within days, a week at most.

The dead didn't interfere; they just waited.

They waited for Lidden Hersch to collapse of a brain aneurysm. They waited for Vikram Sethi to bleed out following an accident with an industrial laser. They waited for Aisha Greer until, sick of wondering what fate they predicted for her, she cut her own throat in a shower stall.

That one clawed at me. Was it suicide, really, if she already knew she was going to die? Or had the dead killed her themselves, with the omen of their presence?

Everyone had heard the stories, but my spot on the shower rota was right after Aisha's. I found her before they were through with her. It didn't look like anything I'd ever seen in a movie back home.

The dead—the stuff they were made of—abandoned their human shapes and *poured* over Aisha like a wave. More accurately, perhaps, like a chemical spill, eating away at her flesh as I watched, then at the bones beneath. I had the anatomy lesson of a lifetime, standing there in my robe with a dissolvable soap pellet in my hand, watching them strip away every layer of Aisha one by one.

When she was broken down all the way, when nothing remained except that primordial ooze that digested and replenished itself, the dead stood back up, and Aisha stood with them.

"Eating enough?" Zophie asked as Ave came back from the bathroom. "You haven't gained much weight the last few weeks." Her eyes were big and shiny, her hair disheveled, but Ave didn't seem to notice.

"I don't have any appetite," they said. "This thing inside me takes up so much room."

"Wait until it clears out," Zophie teased. "You'll be asking for triple servings of every meal."

Ave's due date was two weeks away, and everything was going perfectly. The fetus was head-down, in position and ready to be born.

"Healthy as a house," Zophie concluded, patting Ave's hand before gathering her things to leave. That idiom didn't sound quite right to me, but I didn't say anything.

I walked Zophie to the door and touched her shoulder as she left our quarters.

She didn't meet my eyes as she said goodbye. I watched as she slipped out into the hallway, shrinking against the wall so she wouldn't accidentally touch the teeming green surface of what wasn't quite Aisha. Zophie's glance over her shoulder was like a hunted animal, desperate and despairing, and my heart twisted, imagining what it would be like to hear those gentle, wet footsteps at my back.

But Aisha didn't follow Zophie. She stayed where she was, motionless to the eye yet not at all still, fixed like a sentry before the door to our living quarters.

Funerals on the Ark were a brief, quiet affair, rendered surreal by the fact that the person you were mourning might wander by at any moment.

Sometimes the dead lay quiet, melting back into the organic sludge of the Life Cycle System, but just as often they meandered through the halls, making everyone nervous. But it was only when one fell into step behind you that you knew you were doomed.

The dead couldn't be killed or harmed in any way, since they weren't really bodies, just aggregates of microscopic life temporarily shaped like a human. Fists, knives, and lasers passed through them, all equally harmless; they either collapsed into puddles and reconstituted later, or simply wove themselves back together around the injury. Maybe incineration would have worked, or ejection from the vessel, but as uncanny and awful as the things were, they were still made of nutrients and water—things a closed system like ours couldn't afford to throw away.

"Oh, good," I said, resting my forehead against the cool inside of the door, which looked like wood but felt like metal. "This wasn't stressful enough."

Ave was already going to be the first human being in history to give birth in space, and I was only doing a middling job of not freaking the fuck out about that from moment to moment. Now the physical embodiment of death and decay stood outside our home like we owed her money.

"What'd you say, Magda?" said Ave. Thankfully, the tone in their voice meant they were only half-asking, and would only half-listen to my answer.

"Nothing," I said. They hummed a noncommittal response.

I couldn't tell them. I couldn't let them know there was a corpse-shaped algae bloom waiting to ambush us—saying, without speaking a word, that in a matter of days, one of us would die.

That night, I lay stiff and terrified next to Ave, running through nightmare scenarios in my mind. A thousand ways Ave or the baby could die in labor: postpartum hemorrhage, eclampsia, aspirated meconium, infection. Labor could stall, and in transporting Ave to the medical deck, we could take a wrong turn and fall into the incinerator. Or maybe I was destined to just have a mishap with a kitchen knife, spilling blood all over the floor where Ave would slip and fall in it, triggering early labor.

Maybe Ave should give birth on the medical deck, I thought. Maybe we should schedule a C-section, right now, and to hell with all our plans for a gentle home birth. Maybe we could slip out of our quarters in the dead of night and be back with a premature but living baby in our arms before Aisha realized we'd gone.

But Aisha wasn't here to kill us, I reminded myself. Only to recycle what was left afterward. Even if we could evade her, it didn't mean we'd escape the fate she foretold.

Confronting the inevitability of death is not a relaxing way to wind down before bed. It hurts, like running into a window you thought was a doorway. Ave murmured and shifted in their sleep, unable to get comfortable for long with a fetus on their kidneys—and perhaps, too, absorbing some of my nervous energy. My brain scratched at the problem like a magpie trying to solve a Rubik's cube until, still tense, I fell asleep.

When I woke up, I felt slightly better, in that I was still despondent and terrified, but refreshed enough to get up and go through the motions of my day. The tenacious little bird of my subconscious had pecked away at the puzzle all night, and it might not be any closer to solved, but somehow it looked less terrifying.

The most important thing, my sleeping mind had decided, was that Ave not worry. Whatever was going to happen was going to happen, but there was no reason to burden them with that knowledge.

Someone was going to die in our compartment. I supposed it could still be Zophie, or one of the Ark's medical staff who would be on call during Ave's labor, but that seemed wrong to hope for.

Instead, I would just hope it was me.

The thought that I might have only days left to live—that I might never have a chance to hold our baby in my arms—was so gutting that all I could do was push it to the back of my mind. Today, I was alive, and as long as that stayed true, my job was to take care of Ave. If at all possible, I had to allow them to give birth with a clear, focused mind, far from any bad omens that might distract them.

AN EVENTUAL FEAST

Which meant, in practical terms, that I needed to keep Ave in our compartment until the birth, so they wouldn't lay eyes on Aisha. Their due date was two weeks away. I thought with Zophie's help and a little luck, I could probably contrive to keep them from crossing our threshold until then. Living quarters aboard the Ark were designed to meet almost any physical or emotional need, except for space, and we both often went days without leaving.

Beside me, Ave stirred, grumbled. I leaned over and kissed them on the shoulder.

Ave's eyes popped open. They squinted up at me, disoriented. "Ummh? What—Magda?"

"Shh, sweetheart. Go back to sleep."

They pushed themself halfway up to sitting. Then their face went pale, and they gripped my forearm.

"Ave?" I said. "Are you okay?"

Bizarrely, they laughed. "Yeah," they said slowly. "I mean, no, but yeah. I think—Magda, I think that was a contraction."

Well, at least I don't have to worry about keeping them in our quarters for two weeks, I thought as I frantically tried to buzz Zophie. I kept typing her number wrong. Half the ship would know that my spouse was in labor by the time I finally got hold of our midwife.

"Keep breathing," I reminded Ave as I tried again.

"Yeah, I haven't forgotten how to *breathe,*" Ave said. They were making a cup of tea, even though I kept trying to convince them to sit back down. "I'm in labor, sweetheart, I'm not in a coma."

A horrifically vivid mental image of Ave, unconscious in a hospital bed, flashed across my eyes. What would Aisha and the dead think about a coma patient? A body with no brain activity—would it trigger their instinct to consume? Was that what they were here for?

I rubbed a hand over my eyes. "I know. I'm sorry," I said. "I'm nervous."

"Don't be nervous," Ave said. They said that to me a lot, a testament to the triumph of optimism over experience. "I'm having a baby. This is great. It's normal. People have been doing it for thousands of years."

I nodded. I didn't say the thing we both knew: No one had ever done it in space before.

Neither did I say the thing that only I knew: One of us was marked for death. Ave would find that out soon enough.

Zophie bustled into our quarters without knocking, opening the door just enough to slip through and close it swiftly behind her. *Thank you*, I mouthed over Ave's head.

"I swear, that elevator knew I was in a hurry and kept me waiting on purpose," she said cheerfully. She hugged me, then went to Ave. "Blood pressure and fetal heartbeat, my dear."

As they chatted and checked Ave's vitals, I drifted toward the door and snuck a glance outside. There was Aisha, closer than before.

As I watched, her head cocked at a slight angle, turning as though she were searching for something. Her eyes weren't really eyes, I knew—just the same seething, bubbling green stuff that made up the rest of her body. She couldn't see, not in the way living people did.

But she looked straight at me.

I jumped back from the door, biting my lip just in time to hold in a shriek.

Still, Ave's head snapped around. "What is it?" they asked.

"Nothing," I said. "I was just—"

"Oh, son of a bitch, here it comes," Ave said, bracing themself on the back of a chair.

I dashed to support them, and in that contraction's moaning and cursing, my stumble at the door was temporarily forgotten.

Ave circled the compartment, pacing and bellowing. All very normal, Zophie reassured me, and progressing quickly but safely. Every time Ave winced or cried out, I tensed up and glanced toward the door, but Zophie placed a cool hand on my shoulder and reminded me to relax. I rubbed Ave's back and through their contractions.

"Low and open," Zophie reminded them, and then we all hummed a long, low note together.

"How are you doing?" I asked Ave, brushing hair out of their eyes.

"I love you, honey, but don't fucking touch me right now," they said. "You're a goddamn furnace."

They had been complaining of being too hot for at least an hour, but the climate control in our quarters was already at its lowest temperature setting. Our ventilation just wasn't up to the physical exertion of birth.

"Maybe a cool washcloth for your face," Zophie suggested, but Ave was already shaking their head.

"I need to go for a walk," they said. "I think I'll do a lap around the conservatory, get some breathing room."

My pulse was a hammer in my chest. If Ave walked out the door, they'd see Aisha, and everything would go to hell.

AN EVENTUAL FEAST

They'd panic. Labor would stall, and the risk of complications would climb by the minute. Maybe that was why Aisha was here—because Ave was going to lose the baby.

No, goddammit. I squeezed my eyes shut.

"I don't think you should," I said, trying to keep my tone light. "Your contractions are getting stronger. What if it hurts too much to walk, and you can't get back?"

"I can always call a med cart," said Ave.

"Those things jolt you around so much—" I started. Desperation was creeping into my voice.

"Magda, you're freaking out," Ave said gently. "We talked about this. I need you to stay calm, okay? People go for walks while they're in labor. It's normal. I'm not going to wander off into the wilderness and get eaten by a bear. We're on a spaceship." I flinched at the words *get eaten*. "If I fall down, someone will help me get back. I'm going for a walk, and you're going to stay here and drink a glass of water and try to unwind, okay?"

Without waiting for my answer, they turned, crossed our tiny living space in two steps, and opened the door.

"Zophie, make her drink water," they said over their shoulder, and stepped into the empty hallway.

Aisha was gone.

"What the fuck," I gasped.

Was it safe to feel relieved? Was she really gone? Had it all been some kind of mistake? I ran to the door and looked down the hall. There was only Ave, walking slowly and ponderously, stopping every few meters to catch their breath and wait out another contraction. No harbinger of doom in the shape of Aisha Greer, who had once been my friend.

I turned back into the compartment, my mouth forming the shape of the words 'It's okay,' when I heard Zophie curse and a glass of water—the one Ave had told her to get for me—splash to the floor.

Aisha was inside my home. She stood perfectly still beside the table on which Zophie's implements were arrayed, looking like she'd been there for hours.

"No," I pleaded. "No, stop it. Get out of here."

Aisha said nothing, did nothing, made no sign to acknowledge me. Her chest did not even rise and fall. It's incredibly uncanny, to stand that close to something visibly alive, yet unbreathing.

"Fuck you," I snarled, and in an incoherent act of rage I swung my fist at Aisha's face. It was like punching wet moss. My fist squashed into and through her cheek, which wasn't a cheek—there was no bone underneath, no layers of skin and fat and muscle, just the crawling sameness of that green fungus. It retracted a little, as though trying to get out of my way, completely unlike how human flesh would respond to a blow.

But the worst part was the warmth. I *knew* the walking dead were alive—human effigies constructed of plant life—but somehow in my hindbrain I had expected them to be cold. Aisha's face was as warm as bathwater.

I yanked my hand back, gagging. The expression on Aisha's face, or rather the arrangement of tiny organisms imitating her face, did not change.

Zophie grabbed my shoulders and steered me into a chair.

"You are not helping," she said, very sternly. I hadn't known she was capable of speaking with a tone that sharp.

"She needs to get out of here," I said. "If Ave sees her—"

"We can't make them do anything they're not already doing, so drop it," said Zophie. "She was in here before you opened the door. She came *under* it. If you try to move her, she's going to slip through your fingers. Stop trying to fix something you can't change and start getting yourself under control. Ave needs you to hold it together."

"She's here for one of us," I said, staring down at my hands because I couldn't look at either Zophie or Aisha.

"Could be," Zophie said back. "You used to drive down the street every day not knowing whether a semi truck would plow straight into you. Put it out of your mind."

"I never learned to drive." She raised her eyebrows. "How are you so fucking calm?" I snapped. "The other day when she followed you here, you were an anxious mess."

Zophie shrugged. "Ave's in labor. I can compartmentalize. No one likes to say this, Magda, but death is always in the room during a childbirth. We just try not to look straight at it."

I dropped my head into my hands and took a few deep breaths. "Okay. Okay. Shit, okay."

I could do this, I told myself. I could be strong for Ave, for our baby, even though every nerve in my body was singing an aria of mortal terror. God, I didn't want to be strong. I wanted to scream and cry and hide until someone else fixed it. For an insane moment, I actually missed my mother.

The door clicked open and Ave stood there. "Made it about ten steps before— oh, *fuck me*." Their eyes locked on Aisha, and the look of devastation on their face

    AN EVENTUAL FEAST

was absolute. I briefly thought they were so scared they'd lost bladder control.

Then I realized, of course, that wasn't the case. Ave's water had broken. That's why they had come back. Zophie had explained to us that broken water doesn't mark the beginning of labor like it does in movies; it happens much later in the process and means things are kicking into high gear.

"Ignore her," Zophie said, and I thought she meant me. But of course, she was telling Ave not to focus on Aisha. "We don't know why she's here and we can't do anything about it, so just let it go. Magda, help them get out of their coveralls."

"But—" Ave was cut off by another contraction. Labor, I was realizing, made an excellent excuse for avoiding difficult conversations.

Zophie covered our mattress with a waterproof sheet, and we helped Ave onto the bed. Instead of lying down, they rocked on their hands and knees.

"Does that feel better, love?" I asked.

"No," they snarled.

"Beautiful," said Zophie. "You're doing perfect."

I didn't know what to do with my hands. I didn't know what to do with *myself.* My partner was grunting in animal pain, and a compost pile in the shape of a

woman was waiting to devour whichever one of us died first. My brain clawed at its walls like a caged bird.

Zophie rubbed my arm. "Take a deep breath," she said quietly. "Go get them a cup of water."

A task I could accomplish, at last! I darted for the sink, spilling half the water in my rush on the way back. I held it to Ave's lips and they drank frantically, gulping as much as possible before the next contraction hit.

When I looked back at Aisha, she was closer to Ave. A scream burned my throat, but I held it back.

My partner. My child. I had left my birth planet far behind, no return trip possible. Here on this bed was the whole of my world, and the specter of death loomed over.

A pair of sharp, heavy scissors lay on the table beside the rest of Zophie's tools. They were for cutting the umbilical cord, I knew, a thick flesh cable pulsing with blood. While no one was looking, while Ave wept and rocked on the bed, I ran my hand over their cool steel.

It had to be me, didn't it? I couldn't let Aisha take Ave, or the baby—our hope for the future. Not just ours but everyone's hope, a living prayer that the Ark and everyone aboard were not a doomed branch on humanity's withering tree.

Aisha came to eat something dead. Maybe if I gave her that, she would leave.

I went to the door and peered out into the hall. The other zombies were lined up outside our compartment, teeming with the life that feeds on death, verdant with decay. I recognized Vikram and Lidden, but there were more, five or six of them.

Waiting. Waiting for one of us. Waiting for a death in my family.

Ave *screamed*. I was back by their side in an instant. Zophie murmured encouragement as Ave groaned and swore into the mattress.

"The baby's right there," Zophie crooned. "Just a few more big pushes. You're doing so well. Deep breath, and—"

I inhaled in unison with them, thinking selfishly, as Ave wailed in agony, *I hope it doesn't hurt too much.*

"Magda," Ave said. "*Magda.*"

"I'm here," I said, and followed it with a lie: "I'm not going anywhere."

"Crowning," said Zophie. "Ave, you can put your hand right here and feel your baby's head."

Tears rolled down my face. Ave, on their hands and knees, was weeping a salt puddle onto the plastic sheet covering our bed.

"It hurts," they said. "It hurts, I can't—"

"You can," I said quietly, and kissed their bare, sweaty shoulder. "You are."

Aisha was right beside me now, close enough to touch. Whatever I was going to do, I needed to do it soon. Now. My heart pounded in my throat.

Ave's voice hit a note higher than I'd ever heard, held it—held it—held it until I felt my skull would shatter—and it broke into a sob and Zophie said, "Here they are!"

For a numb, senseless moment I thought she was talking about Ave—where else would they be?—but then I looked, and she was holding something tiny and squirming and bloody.

"Oh," I said. "Oh my God."

I froze in place. Every cell of me yearned to reach for the baby, but I had to grab the scissors or lose my chance forever.

The baby gasped, then wailed, a small but powerful sound. My arms stretched toward them without conscious thought. Ave was panting and crying, trying to turn over and see.

Aisha began to sing.

The sound had no place in this room, no place in this time, no place in my entire understanding of the world, but still, I recognized it as a song in the first instant.

AN EVENTUAL FEAST

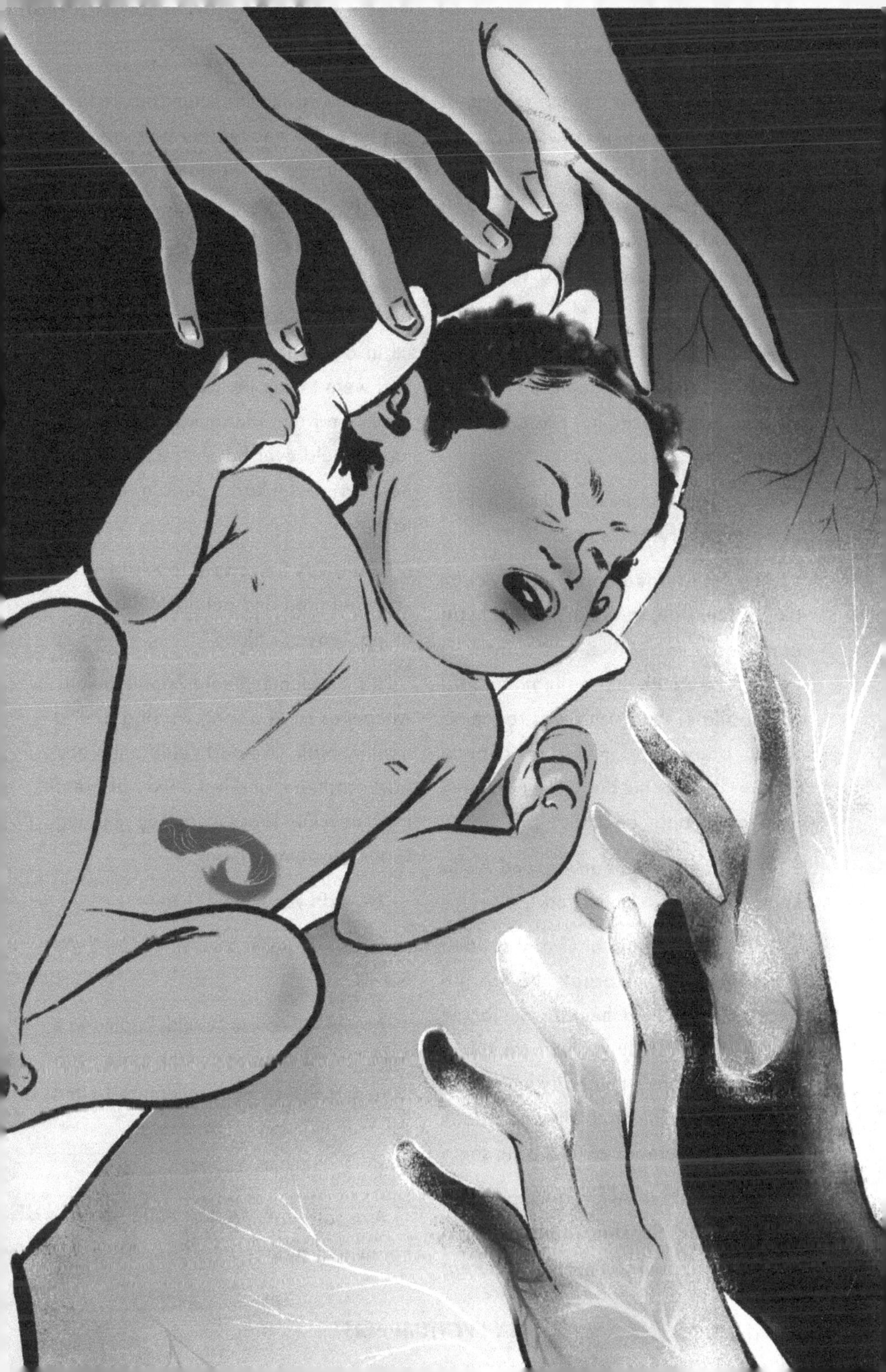

It did not sound like a human voice—it did not come from lungs or vocal chords, since Aisha had none—but it was some kind of vibration, rising and falling in unmistakable melody, emanating from the core of her green and endlessly dying body.

Aisha sang, and stretched her hands out toward the baby, palms up. After a second, I recognized her posture as the mirror of my own.

"No," I said, but my voice disappeared in the thrum of Aisha's song.

Ave, half-turned and lying awkwardly on their side, stared at me with huge, confused eyes. My heart shattered inside of me with the realization that I was too late, that Aisha was reaching for the baby, I had missed my chance, she was here for the baby, she had been here for the baby all along.

The baby kept screaming, and Aisha kept singing. No one moved.

Finally, carefully, as if any sudden movements might break the fragile peace, Zophie held the baby out for me to take. I accepted them with trembling hands. The baby's tiny body was sticky and warm and loud and alive. They took a shuddering breath, and I did the same.

Zophie helped Ave rearrange themself, adjusting the bed so it supported them as they lay back, and I just kept staring down into that scrunched, reddening face. The heavy gray-pink cord lay around the baby's shoulders like a shawl.

It dawned on me that the song I was hearing came not only from Aisha, but from all around me. I turned my head and saw that the other dead had joined us in our warm, humid compartment, and were taking up the eerie yet oddly familiar refrain. The sound was like nothing I would ever have described as a harmony, but it had a certain rightness to it.

"Go away," Ave said to Aisha. They sounded tired and petulant. "No one's dying. Leave us alone."

"It's a welcome," said Zophie quietly. "Midwives have a song we sing after a healthy birth. Like part celebration and part gratitude, and just a way of greeting a new life. That's what they're doing. That's why they're here."

"How do you know?" I said.

She shrugged expressively. "Can't you feel it?"

I could. Of course I could. Zophie was right. The song Aisha and the other dead were singing—my body recognized it and sang along in its own, silent way.

"It's beautiful," said Zophie.

Ave said nothing, just held out their hands and scooped the baby out of my

AN EVENTUAL FEAST

grasp, holding our child squalling and wriggling to their chest.

I took deep breaths, trying to lean into the song, trying to let the terror flow out of me. It was all right. Everything was all right. The baby and Ave and I were alive, and the green things—whatever they were—had come to praise us, not to bury us. In their unknowable way, they had predicted the beginning of a life instead of the end of one.

Or perhaps, from their vantage point, it was all the same.

I looked at Ave, guiding the baby's mouth to their nipple, and I felt a joy and awe and fear so huge, I didn't know how to touch it. The shadows of the dead fell across their perfect, living bodies.

My family was beautiful and alive, there amidst the choir of death. We were, all of us, part of this song. We would all have to sing it, someday.

GUEST EDITOR-IN-CHIEF

HAILEY PIPER is the author of horror books *The Worm and His Kings*, *Unfortunate Elements of My Anatomy*, and *Benny Rose, the Cannibal King*. She's an active member of the Horror Writers Association and author of over sixty published short stories, to be found in places such as *Year's Best Hardcore Horror*, *Dark Matter Magazine*, *Daily Science Fiction*, *The Arcanist*, *Tales to Terrify*, and multiple times in beloved *Planet Scumm*. Hailing from the haunted woods of New York, she now lives with her wife in Maryland, where their paranormal research is highly classified.

Find Hailey at haileypiper.com, or on Twitter via @HaileyPiperSays.

UPCOMING PUBLICATIONS

Hailey's debut novel *Queen of Teeth*, a queer body horror love story, releases from Rooster Republic Press in August '21. It has been called "one of the best horror books of 2021" by Rue Morgue, and "a powerful, beautiful horror story" by Kirkus Reviews in a starred review. She also has work upcoming in *Cast of Wonders*, *Vastarien*, and several anthologies.

EDITOR'S CHOICE

» Reading: *Annihilation* by Jeff Vandermeer
» Watching: *Godzilla: Singular Point*
» Listening to: playlists prominently ft. Kate Bush

COVER + SPOT ILLUSTRATOR

MAURA "MOE" MCGONAGLE is an illustrator, a writer, and a freshly minted editor with a passion for story telling. They specialize in narrative works and have created pieces for all ages, aiming to create dynamic, inclusive literature.

They got their start working collaboratively and were featured in 'Being True, an LGBTQ Anthology', the *Bar Crawl Anthology*, and was the illustrator for Brandon Sichling's *'Touched by Fire'*.

Focused on vibrant creative stories with immersive art, they try not to limit themselves to one genre and instead embrace layered narratives that range the full spectrum of human emotion.

They can be found on twitter and patreon, both at @doingartiguess, or in the wild, probably lost.

PROJECTS TO WATCH

Maura was one of the creative leads—along with Renie Jesanis and Liz Y—behind 'Starbound, a Science Fiction Anthology,' a succesfully crowd-funded comic collection produced by Boston Comics Roundtable.

They also work with a team to produce the ongoing long-form comic series, 'WITCH'— a story of three sisters guiding their newest member through the twists and turns of being a witch. New installments can be found on Webtoons.

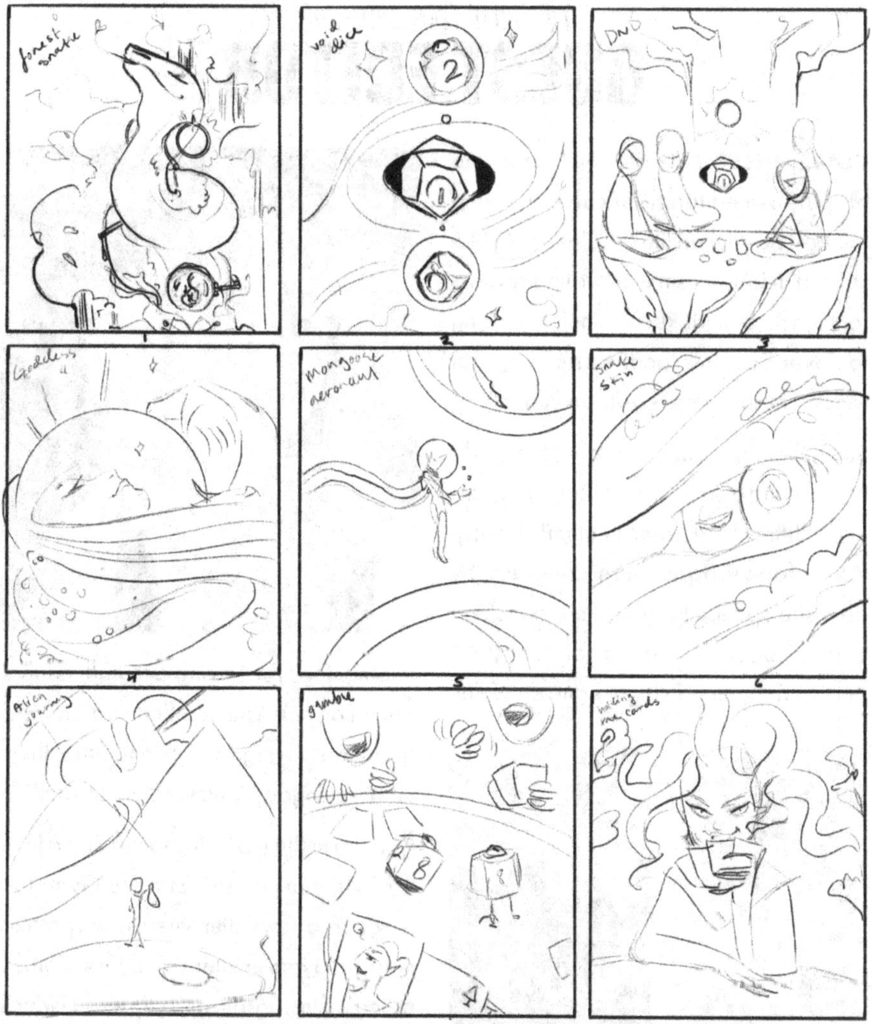

COVER DESIGN

"The idea for the cover was to capture the idea that gender is something to contemplate. It's a journey, it's not fixed, It's a challenge to meet every day. But not in a negative way—that's essential.

It's an act of creation, a push and pull with the universe creating this beautiful, multi-dimensional dance that's asking the question *what will you be today?*"

GUEST EDITOR

CLARE FULLER is a writer, illustrator, and all-purpose editorialista currently living her best bewitched life in Salem, MA. She started in journalism with writing reviews for Funeral Sounds Records before moving to cover Boston's local music scene for Massachusetts staple, *Allston Pudding*.

Since then, she's been tackling the world of print and paper with editorial projects, like editing for *Planet Scumm!* A copywriter for an agriculture company by day, she spends her free time sketching comics, beach-combing for sea glass, and marathoning Twilight Zone episodes.

Submissions *for Saving Daylight* Issue 3 open Fall '21. You can find info on Instagram at @savingdaylightzine or hit them up at savingdaylightzine@gmail.com!

If you're in the mood for something a little trashier, you can subscribe to *Gym, Tan, Languish*, a newsletter where Clare profiles major players in internet culture. Follow along on Instagram at @clare.psd (which is mostly just a collection of Photoshop portraits of the Vanderpump Rules cast).

She is Editor-in-Chief of *Saving Daylight*, an independent arts magazine about seasonal depression, founded in 2019. Each issue highlights writing and visual art about dealing with mental health during the gloomy ides of winter. $5 from each sale goes to a charity supporting therapy resources for underfunded communities.

She's a firm believer in blurring the space between high-brow and low-brow, because life is too short for "guilty" pleasures (literary symposiums are cool and all, but you ever watch Andy Cohen mediate a season reunion for Real Housewives of New York? Pure art.)

THE ONLY DIFFERENCE BETWEEN AN OLD SPOT ILLUSTRATION AND COMEDY GOLD IS YOUR CAPTION!

This Tyler Berd original crawled out from the back of the archive, all the way from Issue #2 of *Planet Scumm*, "Tales from the Unspeakable Thumb Drive."

Aren't you lucky, Reader? We've revived it just for you!

YOUR CAPTION:

____

____

____

SUBMIT YOUR CAPTION AT PLANETSCUMM.SPACE/CAPTIONS!

The top two entries will be voted on through the Planet Scumm instagram and one chosen jokester will win an annual subscription of three books.

Must be 13 or older to enter. Up to three entries per person. Contest ends October 15, 2021.